THE REGULATOR

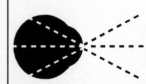

THE REGULATOR

ETHAN J. WOLFE

THORNDIKE PRESS

A part of Gale, Cengage Learning

GALE
CENGAGE Learning·

Farmington Hills, Mich • San Francisco • New York • Waterville, Maine
Meriden, Conn • Mason, Ohio • Chicago

Copyright © 2015 by Ethan J. Wolfe.
Thorndike Press, a part of Gale, Cengage Learning.

Thorndike Press® Large Print Western.
The text of this Large Print edition is unabridged.
Other aspects of the book may vary from the original edition.
Set in 16 pt. Plantin.

LIBRARY OF CONGRESS CATALOGING-IN-PUBLICATION DATA

Wolfe, Ethan J.
  The regulator / by Ethan J. Wolfe. — Large print edition.
    pages cm. — (Thorndike Press large print western)
    ISBN 978-1-4104-8311-9 (hardcover) — ISBN 1-4104-8311-8 (hardcover)
    1. Forensic pathologists—Fiction. 2. Serial murder investigation—Fiction. 3. United States—History—Civil War, 1861-1865—Veterans—Fiction. 4. Large type books. I. Title.
PS3612.A5433R44 2015b
813'.6—dc23   2015019548

Published in 2015 by arrangement with Ethan J. Wolfe

Printed in Mexico
1 2 3 4 5 6 7 19 18 17 16 15

THE REGULATOR

ONE

William R. Burke left the White House shortly after eight in the morning after a breakfast meeting with the President. Garfield had been in sour spirits and barely touched the lavish breakfast prepared for him by the White House staff. At the conclusion of the meeting, Garfield gave Burke a file marked *Top Secret* with orders to burn the file after reading it.

The meeting was just as sour in Burke's opinion, but Garfield was the President and his opinion was the only one in the room that counted.

Burke's carriage waited for him outside the White House gates. He could have walked to Congress if the chilly morning in mid-April had been warmer, but the temperature was right around forty degrees and he'd recently recovered from a nasty winter cold.

Burke told the driver to ride around for a

while before driving to Congress. He needed time to read the file that was ten or twelve pages thick. After reading each page twice, the carriage arrived at Congress shortly after nine a.m.

Burke left instructions for the driver to wait and then climbed the steps into the hallowed halls of Congress. He went directly to the cafeteria for a cup of coffee and to read the file a third time.

A few dozen senators and congressmen lingered in the giant eating hall for what they referred to as *Power Meetings.*

Burke took a table far in the back so he could sit alone and read. He read and took two sips from the cup and when he was done reading and took a third sip the coffee was cold.

The cafeteria was empty when Burke exited and took a hallway to the office of Congressman Murphy, a first-termer from Tennessee. Even though he had read the file three times, Burke wasn't prepared for the sight of the man when he knocked on the door and Murphy answered it himself.

Burke stood five-foot-eleven inches tall in stocking feet, a good four inches taller than the average man. Murphy, at least six-foot-three, towered over him. His dark hair was shoulder length and speckled with gray, as was his beard, making it impossible to tell his age by his appearance.

"Yes?" Murphy said in a deep, resonating voice.

"Congressman Murphy?" Burke asked.

"Yes, what do you want?" Murphy asked with slight impatience.

"I'm William R. Burke, Special Assistant to the President," Burke said.

Murphy's steel gray eyes seemed to look right through Burke and Burke felt the hairs on the back of his neck stand up.

"Okay, so what do you want?" Murphy asked. "I'm due on the floor in thirty minutes."

"No, no, you're not," Burke said.

Murphy's gray eyes narrowed to slits. "Why not?"

"Because I'm here on request of the President and we need to talk," Burke said.

"I was just about to have coffee, want a cup?"

"Yes."

"Come in. Close the door. Grab a chair."

Burke closed the door and took a chair opposite Murphy's desk.

"Milk and sugar?" Murphy asked as he went behind his desk and picked up the pot sent over by the cafeteria staff.

"Yes, thank you."

Murphy filled two mugs with coffee, sugar, and cream and set one before Burke.

"You got five minutes to explain before I toss you out of my office," Murphy said as he took his chair.

"Then you'd be tossing the President out of your office, Congressman." Burke said, somewhat taken aback.

Murphy took a small sip from his cup and looked at Burke. "You've just used up four of your five minutes. Go."

"Are you aware, sir, that I represent the President?" Burke asked. "That if you threaten me, you threaten him. I could have his Secret Service place you in . . ."

"Don't tell me about the Secret Service, Mr. Burke," Murphy said. "I was handpicked by Grant as his personal bodyguard when he created the damn thing. So what does the President want? I wasn't aware that he knew I existed."

"Oh, he knows," Burke said. "And that's why he sent me to see you."

Murphy looked at the file on Burke's lap.

"Is that file about me?" Murphy asked.

"Yes."

Murphy took a sip from his cup, then opened a desk drawer and removed a pipe and tobacco pouch. "So what does the

President want?" he asked as he stuffed the bowl.

"You are aware of the expansion taking place out west?" Burke asked. "With settlers, the railroads, mining operations, and government. Many territories wish to apply for statehood, but in order for that to happen, there must be economic growth and population growth and civilization and law and order."

"You're taking the long road when the short path will do," Murphy said as he struck a match and lit his pipe.

Burke took a sip of coffee. He sighed softly and took a shallow breath. "There is a crisis out there that has shut down the expansion of the Santa Fe Railroad, settlements, and mining. The President is assigning you, and only you, to handle it. Your term in office is up in eight months and you will resign early to be reappointed to the Secret Service answerable only to the President. This is highly classified and absolutely top secret."

"Top Secret. That's what it reads in my file, doesn't it?" Murphy asked. "Is it such a secret that you won't tell me what it is I'm supposed to handle for the President?"

Burke felt beads of sweat appear on his forehead. "About six months ago somebody started murdering railroad workers, new

11

settlers, and miners along the expansion of the Santa Fe and the new territories opened by the government for settlers and mining operations."

"Somebody?" Murphy asked. "Or more than one somebodies?"

"We don't know."

"And I suppose you don't know why?"

"No."

"What do the local sheriffs, marshals, and the Army say about it?"

Burke shook his head and beads of sweat rolled down his face. He took a moment to use a napkin from the desk to wipe it away. "Local sheriffs, marshals, and railroad police have no idea who is behind the murders. The President doesn't want to involve the Army as this assignment is, as I said, classified."

"How many victims?"

"Thirty, fifty, more, I just don't know."

"And I'm supposed to do exactly what?"

"Go west, find the killer or killers, and put a stop to it."

"Kill him is what you mean," Murphy said.

"As the President said to me this morning, end it with extreme prejudice."

Murphy looked at Burke and Burke felt his shirt stick to his back. It was quite clear why the President chose Murphy for the assignment; the man had the look of a stone-cold killer in his cold dead eyes.

"Extreme prejudice," Murphy said.

"That's what he said."

"What if I say no?"

"The country can't afford for information to become common knowledge," Burke said. "Settlers won't move west and add to the population. The railroad won't expand to the routes necessary for the delivery of cattle to markets, mail delivery will slow, and territories won't become states and so on. People like J.P. Morgan and William Henry Vanderbilt are behind most of these projects and their decisions affect the expansion and development of the country. The President and the country need you to put a stop to these murders for the benefit of all."

"Benefit of the President is what you mean," Murphy said.

"As the President goes so goes everything else," Burke said. "Look, let's be honest. As a first term, junior congressman from Tennessee your impact on the country as a whole is next to nothing. Hell, your attitude around here has made it almost impossible to win reelection, so why not make a real difference in the country and take this assignment?"

"What's wrong with my attitude?"

"You scare the shit out of people, for one thing," Burke said. "You're scaring the shit out of me right now, and all we're doing is sitting and having coffee."

Murphy took a sip from his cup and then puffed on his pipe. "I get the feeling it doesn't take much to scare the shit out of you, Mr. Burke."

"That's not an answer."

"That doesn't make me wrong."

"I need to give the President an answer within the hour."

"What's my compensation?"

"Your what?"

"My compensation," Murphy said. "You're asking me to leave my seat and forfeit my salary, so what is my compensation for taking on this assignment?"

"I don't know. It didn't come up."

"Well, here it is then," Murphy said. "I have eight months left in my term. I will be paid in full for those eight months, plus another two years' worth of my salary as congressman for forfeiting my reelection. This money will be deposited in my bank back home in Tennessee. I will require twenty thousand dollars in expense money paid before I leave. I want my full identification returned to me as it was when Grant left office. My compensation is not negotiable. Go tell the President that and then get back to me."

Burke stared at Murphy.

"I wasn't asking," Murphy said.

Burke stood up and started for the door.

"One more thing," Murphy said.

Burke turned around.

"I make no apologies for my conduct or my temperament," Murphy said. "Remember that if you give me reason to lose it."

Burke nodded, opened the door, and left Murphy at his desk.

On the ride back to the White House, Burke scanned the file one more time to commit it to memory.

Born to a Tennessee whiskey maker, Murphy was well educated when he joined the Union Army and was given the rank of First Lieutenant. After proving himself worthy in battle, he was promoted to Captain. Served with Grant until sixty-three when he was assigned to spearhead a special sniper squad. In early sixty-four he was recalled by Grant and given a new assignment and promotion to Major. The assignment was to lead his special squad across the south and kill anything and everything wearing gray.

No official statistics were kept, but it's estimated Murphy killed over two hundred men during that assignment.

After the war Murphy retired as a full Colonel and returned to his father's whiskey-making business.

In 1870 Murphy was called to Washington by President Grant and at the request of Grant became part of the newly formed US Secret Service and Grant's personal bodyguard. Murphy served in this post until Grant left office in 1877.

In 1877 Murphy returned to Tennessee and ran for Congress and won the junior seat and once again found himself in Washington.

Burke looked out the window of the carriage.

"Killed more than two hundred men," he said aloud.

"Did you say something, Mr. Burke?" the driver asked from outside the carriage.

"Pull over and stop for a moment," Burke said.

The driver slowed to a stop on the side of the road. Murphy got out, stepped away from the carriage, drew a match, and set fire to the file. Only when it had burned to ashes did Burke return to the carriage.

■ ■ ■ ■

Murphy was at his desk on the floor of
Congress, listening to the idiot from Mas-
sachusetts drone on about something that
was so tedious he tuned the man out
completely.

A Page, all of thirteen, entered through
his designated hallway and quietly dropped
a note on Murphy's desk.

The note was from Burke. He was waiting
in Murphy's office.

Murphy stood up and followed the Page
out of the hall, left the boy at his station,
and returned to his office.

Burke was looking out the window when
Murphy opened his office door and stepped
inside.

Burke turned from the window. "The
envelope on your desk has identification and
reports, and twenty thousand dollars inside.
The President wants to know when you
leave for New Mexico to the site of the most
recent murders."

"Did he agree to my salary demands?"

"I wouldn't be here otherwise."

"I'll catch the first express train west
tomorrow."

"Good," Burke said. "Good."

Murphy slid behind his desk, opened a bottom drawer, and removed a bottle of Tennessee whiskey and two glasses. He gave one glass to Burke.

"My father's whiskey," Murphy said.

Burke sniffed and took a sip. "I'll remember it."

"Also remember this," Murphy said. "I won't be used by you, the President, or anyone else, so if you're thinking of some political stunt I advise against it. Otherwise, I'll head west tomorrow and do my best to solve your problem."

Burke downed his whiskey and set the glass on the desk.

"Good day, Mr. Murphy," Burke said.

Murphy waited for Burke to leave the office before he picked up the envelope.

"May I speak freely, Mr. President?" Burke said.

Seated at his desk in the Oval Office, Garfield pointed to a chair and snapped, "For God's sake, man, take a chair."

Burke took one of several chairs opposite the desk.

"What's on your mind, William?" Garfield asked.

"This Murphy, sir. I'm not sure he's the right man for this assignment."

"He's exactly the right man for it," Garfield said.

"But, Mr. President, he's . . ."

"Smart, fearless, and not afraid to pull the trigger or use violence when it's called for," Garfield said. "You didn't serve, did you, William?"

"During the war, no, sir."

"I served with Grant and saw Murphy work firsthand," Garfield said. "He is no one to trifle with, but more importantly he can end this reign of terror out there and the western expansion will move forward in the right direction again."

"But at what cost, sir?"

"Who gives a damn about cost," Garfield said. "No one is going to know about it, anyway. The point is, the progress of this country won't and can't be stopped because one vicious criminal is committing insane acts of violence. Hell, I would send Satan if he were willing to go. No, William, Murphy is exactly the right man for this assignment. Grant would not have selected him for the Secret Service and moved him into the White House was he not."

"I hope to God that you're right, sir," Burke said.

"Don't underestimate Murphy, William," Garfield warned. "He's far more intelligent than he lets on. Now, I have a great deal to do for the meeting this afternoon. See you then."

"One final question?"

"What?"

"In the file you gave me, all references to Murphy give no first or middle name," Burke said. "He's referred to as Captain, Colonel, Congressman, or Agent, but no use of a first name. Would you happen to know it, sir?"

The question gave Garfield pause. "Why, no, I do not," he said. "I'm sure it's in the Congressional Record. Look it up when you have a chance."

"Yes, sir." Burke stood up. "I'll see you at the meeting."

Two

Murphy packed his black trail clothes, boots, extra underwear, and sundries into two large saddlebags and set them aside on the living room floor of the small home he rented in Virginia just over the border from Washington.

From a chest under the bed he removed a .45 Schofield revolver, a .32 belly gun, holsters, and a trail knife and took them to the kitchen table to clean, oil, and load each weapon. The Winchester 75 rifle and Henry rifle were stored in the closet and he took them to the table and did the same. When he packed the rifles away in a long carrying case he added plenty of ammunition.

From his bookcase in the den, Murphy removed publications on science and advances in forensics and took them to the kitchen. He prepared a light dinner and scanned the various publications while he ate.

After dinner he did another check of gear, saddlebags, and luggage and turned in early for he needed to leave before dawn in the morning.

Burke met the senior senator from Tennessee at ten in the evening in the halls of the Library of Congress. His name was Tunney and he was a big Irishman, who in his youth had red hair, but in his old age what was left of his hair was mostly white.

"Thank you for meeting me, Senator," Burke said.

"I don't sleep much anyway these days," Tunney explained. "Old age doesn't agree with me. Shall we sit and you can tell me what's on your mind?"

They walked to a table in the main hall and took seats.

"As I said earlier, I need information on Congressman Murphy," Burke said. "At the request of the President."

"What kind of information?"

"Anything that you know about him. Do you know his first and middle name, for instance?"

Tunney sat back in the chair for a moment. "No, I do not," he said. "I've known his father fifty years, although not well. I've known Murphy for at least since the war, but we've never been what you would call friendly. It must be on file, look it up."

"It isn't."

"He filed papers to run for Congress, didn't he?" Tunney said. "He went to West Point and served on Grant's Secret Service, there must be dozens of documents floating around with his name on them."

"There isn't, or I haven't found any."

Tunney stared at Burke for a moment.

"You didn't call me here at this hour to discuss Murphy's missing first name," he said. "What's really on your mind?"

"I want to know what kind of man he is," Burke said. "I was hoping you could shed some light on him for me."

"For Christ sake, don't they keep records at the White House and the War Department?"

"I'm talking about what's not in the files."

"I see," Tunney said. "Off the record because I have no evidence or facts that prove this story that I heard is true and it could be the figment of someone's imagination. Agreed?"

"Yes."

"Six Union Army deserters riding west in late sixty-four rode through Murphy's property where his wife and young son lived in a farmhouse," Tunney said. "When he wasn't making whiskey at his father's distillery, Murphy operated a two hundred and fifty acre farm not far from the family business. Most deserters stayed away from towns, so when they needed supplies they usually robbed a farmhouse. That's probably the reason they stopped at Murphy's farm. There is no way to know what transpired inside the house, but that night, Murphy's father smelled smoke from miles away and when he arrived at the farmhouse it had burned to the ground with Murphy's wife and son inside."

"My good God," Burke said.

"Mr. Burke, if the story is true, God had little to do with it," Tunney said. "But, there's more. Apparently, when Murphy's father wrote to his son, he never mentioned this tragedy. My guess would be to spare him the pain while still engaged in combat. And as I heard it, after his discharge, when Murphy returned home from the war in late sixty-five and discovered what had happened, he used his influence and located the Army detachment assigned to track deserters. Turns out they were a day's ride behind the men who killed his family. They never caught up to them, but Murphy got the names and descriptions of all six. He spent the next three years tracking those men and caught up to them one at a time and put a bullet in each man's head. The last man was hiding out as a church deacon in a little town in Idaho. Murphy walked in and shot him in the back of the head during the opening hymn in front of a hundred people."

"He killed them all in cold blood?"

"I suppose it's not too difficult to kill in cold blood when inside you yourself are just as dead," Tunney said.

"Did Grant know this story?"

"Aw, hell, Burke, for all I know it was Grant who started the story as a way to put fear into anyone who might try to assassinate him."

Burke was silent for a moment.

"What do you think?" Burke finally asked. "True or false?"

"As I said, the entire story could be the figment of someone's imagination," Tunney said. "But I wouldn't bet against the son of a bitch."

THREE

By oil lamp, Murphy entered the barn and saddled his horse. There was a chill in the air and he placed a heavy wool blanket under the saddle to protect his horse's skin.

It was an hour to daylight and after he walked his horse to the house and tied him to the post, he went inside for a final cup of coffee. He took it black with an ounce of whiskey to take the slight edge off the morning air. He skipped breakfast as it was too early and his stomach wasn't ready for food. He could eat on the train later.

Wearing a black frock coat over his vest, Murphy left the house, mounted his horse, and rode the ten or so miles to Washington to catch the train west. The sun was up and the train was starting to board when he arrived around seven-thirty.

Murphy boarded his horse in the specially designed boxcar to transport horses long distances and then took saddle, saddlebags, and his lone suitcase and gave his ticket to the collector, who took him to his sleeper compartment.

"What time does the dining car open?" Murphy said.

"One hour after the train leaves the station," the collector said. "Around nine or so if we leave on time."

"Is it possible to have something delivered to my room?" Murphy said.

"Costs extra."

"That's fine."

"Fill out the meal card and hang it on the door," the collector said. "A steward will collect it and deliver your breakfast."

Murphy found the menu card on the small dresser and filled it in for a full breakfast and hung it outside the door.

Then he sprawled out on the bed that was just large enough for a man his size and closed his eyes. The trick to falling asleep almost immediately was one he learned during the war out of necessity. Close your eyes and think about nothing, force all thoughts and images from your mind and allow the blackness to take over, and then try to stay awake and sleep follows.

Murphy opened his eyes when a steward knocked on the door with breakfast. Instantly awake, Murphy stood and opened the door and the steward wheeled in a serving trolley. Murphy gave the man a dollar in silver and was instructed to leave the trolley in the hall when he was finished.

Murphy dug out pamphlets, papers, and thin notebooks from his suitcase and spread them out at the table and then served up his breakfast. Scrambled eggs, bacon, baked beans, grits, toast, juice, coffee, apple pie with a slice of cheese.

He read while he ate.

A Czech physiologist in 1823 published a thesis discussing fingerprint patterns, but did not mention the use of prints for identification. In 1853 or so, German Georg von Meissner studied friction ridges on fingers, but it wasn't until 1858 that Sir William Herschel initiated fingerprinting in India. Prints were used on pension documents to prevent collection of money after a pensioner's death. Printing prisoners upon sentencing was used to prevent fraud in serving sentences. In Paris, Paul-Jean Coulier discovered that iodine fumes can reveal fingerprints on paper. Only last year Doctor Henry Faulds suggested to Scotland Yard that police use fingerprints in the course of investigative work, but it was dismissed as claptrap and forgotten.

In the United States, Murphy doubted

one in a thousand people was even aware fingerprints existed.

Finished with breakfast, Murphy took a cup of coffee to the chair by the window, opened the shades for light, and read his notes and periodicals on ballistic fingerprinting. Rifling was simply the grooves made on a bullet when fired through the rifled barrel of a rifle or handgun. Rifling a barrel made the weapon more accurate than a smooth bored weapon and it was discovered later on that each groove was unique to each weapon. In 1835 in England the grooves in a bullet were matched to the grooves in a murder suspect's gun and even though the evidence would not have been allowed in court the murderer confessed. For the last thirty-five years this information has been ignored, dismissed, forgotten, or lost.

Murphy stuffed his pipe, had more coffee, and continued reading. Dentistry had come a long way in the past several decades. It was not that long ago that the only pain medication for pulling a tooth was to get drunk, but advancements in medicine, drugs, and equipment have made the procedure all but painless. In 1692 during the Salem Witch Trials the Reverend Burroughs used to bite his victims. The marks on the victims were compared to his bite marks and it was the first time in the US that bite marks were used to convict someone of a crime. This science was then lost for centuries.

Murphy closed his notes and books, wheeled the cart into the hallway, closed and locked the door, drew the shades, and returned to bed. When he awoke four hours later the train was at a stop to take on coal and water.

He filled the washbasin with water and stuck his entire face into the cold water for sixty seconds. He toweled dry and left the room to walk from car to car to the rear of the train to visit his horse. As luck would have it, his was the only horse stabled in the car even though it was large enough to hold six.

Murphy dug into his pocket for some sugar cubes and patted his horse on the neck while he ate them.

"It's a long ride, Boyle," Murphy said.

He had never officially named him, but he called him Boyle often enough that the horse responded to the word and he turned and looked at Murphy.

There were brushes and combs hung on the wall and Murphy removed a thick brush and spent the next half hour brushing and grooming his horse until his coat gleamed in the dim lighting.

"Now let's have a look," Murphy said.

He lifted the front right leg, bent in backwards, and held it between his knees as he inspected the shoe and hoof for cracks and breaks. Using a small pocket knife he removed dirt and a few small pebbles and then repeated the procedure on the other three legs.

"When we stop long enough I'll take you out for a ride." Murphy gave Boyle a few more cubes and rubbed his neck.

In one of the main riding cars, Murphy read a newspaper while he smoked his pipe. The car was large enough to hold a hundred, but just twenty or so were scattered about in seats.

A porter walked through the car and Murphy stopped him for a moment.

"Will there be any long layovers? I'd like to stretch my horse's legs."

"Tomorrow mid-morning there will be a two-hour stopover for a connecting train in Kansas City, Missouri."

"Thank you."

Murphy finished the newspaper and returned to his sleeper cabin. He didn't carry his gun belt on the train, but he did conceal a small .45 caliber, two-shot der-ringer in a pocket and he set it on the table before stripping down to comfortable underwear.

He filled the pipe with fresh tobacco and continued reading on the bed.

The latest murders took place between Santa Fe, New Mexico, and Dodge City, Kansas, as track was being laid for the con-nection to Kansas City. After a two-year delay in construction in court over land rights, work continued with a fury only to be halted once again when workers refused to work until the murderer was caught.

And who could blame them?

Reports of settlers shot and burned in their covered wagons, railroad workers hung, stabbed, shot, and strangled all across the territory were on everyone's mind and when it touched the railroad, the men shut down and went on strike.

The scope of territory the murders were reported in was massive. Idaho, Montana, Wyoming, Utah, Colorado, Kansas, and New Mexico, and who knew where else?

Murphy pulled out a map from his suitcase and spread it on the bed. He drew a circle around the seven known murder sites and the area was huge. The murderer or murderers traveled extensively to commit their crimes.

Why?

Murphy pulled out a small tablet and pencil and scribbled that down on a blank page.

Then he smoked his pipe, thought, and made notes of random ideas.

Why did he cover so much territory? Out of a need to select the right victims?

Who were the right victims?

Innocent settlers traveling west to start a new life on land purchased from the government below market value so as to increase the population?

Railroad workers trying to connect major cities and ports?

The two seemingly weren't connected.

Settlers and railroad workers, what did they have in common that they both became victims of a bloody rampage?

The two classes of victims were as different as a rich banker and a poor sharecropper.

On the surface.

What was below the surface that connected the two?

Murphy paused long enough to refill his pipe and pour a shot of his father's whiskey into a water glass.

How many total victims to date?

How many are settlers, how many are

railroad workers?

Witnesses?

Any?

Any left alive?

Evidence?

Motive?

Murphy sat back against the pillows and puffed on the pipe.

Motive?

He ruled out robbery.

Jealousy wasn't high on the list as well.

It was difficult to be jealous of a farmer toiling in his fields all day, up at four, to bed at eight, without any guarantee of success. Railroad workers labored seven days a week in all kinds of weather and none of them got rich. Many of them died on the job, were buried and forgotten.

Neither profession, it seemed to Murphy, warranted much envy.

Again, on the surface of things.

Through the centuries man has struggled to understand the insanity of those plagued by that condition. And while very little was known about the insane, disturbed mind, one thing was for certain: whatever conversations and hallucinations they had in their minds were as real to them as the conversation Murphy had ordering breakfast.

Just because you didn't see who they were talking to or hear the voices didn't mean it wasn't happening.

So maybe a voice in someone's head was telling that someone to murder railroad workers and settlers?

Again it came back to why.

Maybe only that someone knew the answer.

Murphy got up and pulled the cord hanging beside the door. He splashed some cold water on his face, dumped the spent tobacco from his pipe, and refilled the bowl. By then there was a soft knock on the door and he opened it.

"You called, sir?" the steward asked.

"Can I get a pot of coffee?"

"Anything else with that?"

"Just coffee for now."

"Ten minutes," the steward said.

Murphy closed the door and sat at the small desk and lit his pipe. He smoked for a while and answered the door when the steward returned with the pot of coffee. He filled a cup, splashed in some whiskey, and looked at his notes.

Jealousy seemed far-fetched and remote.

Revenge.

One of the oldest and original deadly sins.

Revenge against an unfaithful wife, lover, or

husband? Revenge against someone who stole from or cheated you? Or murdered or raped a loved one? There were a hundred or more reasons for revenge.

But revenge against what wrongdoing and against whom?

The railroad?

Settlers moving west?

Murphy closed the tablet and drank some coffee. It didn't make sense. What did railroad workers and settlers have in common with each other? What beef did the killer have against two separate and very remote groups of people that tied together and resulted in the mass murders from both groups?

Two separate serial killers each with a beef against the railroad and settlers that by coincidence happened to overlap each other?

That would be a hell of a coincidence, but made more sense than one individual with grudges against both groups.

Murphy stood, grabbed his coat and derringer, and headed to the gentlemen's car.

The gentlemen's car was occupied with card players, readers, cigar smokers, whiskey drinkers, and small groups talking politics.

Murphy went to the bar and ordered a brandy. He took the small glass to a window seat, sipped, and looked out at the land rolling by. It was difficult to judge the speed of the train by the whirling scenery outside the window. Maybe fifty miles per hour, a good ten miles faster than the fastest horse on a sprint.

The railroad changed the country. Hell, it changed the world. A trip from New York to California took three or more months if you survived it and now could be made in six or seven days, and in total comfort.

Settlers in underpopulated territories were a necessity if the territory were to create a thriving economy, bring law and order to wilderness, create towns, and eventually apply for statehood.

Two separate issues connected by death.

Murphy sipped brandy and turned away from the window when voices became raised and heated at a card table.

Six men were engaged in a game. Five of the men were older, one was younger. The younger man, heated and loud, said, "You're a lying, cheating, son of a bitch," to the man directly opposite him.

"I assure you, sir, that I do not cheat," the older man explained. "I am simply a better card player than you."

"No man beats me six straight times without cheating," the younger man insisted. "Stand up and let me see what

37

you're hiding."

"I'll do no such thing," the older man replied.

The younger man jumped to his feet and pulled the .44 Smith & Wesson from the holster on his right hip and cocked it. "Show me, you son of a bitch," he said.

The bartender started to come around from the bar.

"You stay put, barkeep," the younger man ordered. "This ain't your affair."

The bartender paused and stepped back.

"Now stand up and show me what you got tucked away inside your coat," the younger man said.

The other occupants of the car were silent, focused on the younger man and his .44.

The older man slowly rose to his feet.

The younger man waved the .44. "Open your jacket."

Murphy stood up, pulled the derringer, walked up behind the younger man, and stuck the barrel against the back of the younger man's head.

The younger man froze.

"That's a .45 pressed against your stupid skull," Murphy said and removed the Smith & Wesson from the younger man's hand.

"This ain't your affair," the younger man said.

"I'd ask you to turn around but then you'd see my face and come for me later and I really don't feel like killing a young and stupid person," Murphy said and cracked the younger man on the head with his own gun.

He fell in a heap across the table.

Murphy looked at the bartender. "You have railroad police aboard?"

The bartender nodded.

"Get them. Have them lock this idiot up," Murphy said.

Murphy stuck the derringer in his pocket and walked out of the car.

Murphy was on his bed lost in thought when there was a knock on the door and a voice said, "Mr. Murphy, are you in there, sir?"

Murphy got up and opened the door.

A wide man dressed in a suit looked at him. He held a wallet with a badge for Murphy to look at.

"Kevin Meeks, railroad police. May I come in for a moment?"

Murphy stepped aside.

Meeks entered and Murphy closed the door.

"That was a memorable stunt you pulled in the gentlemen's car," Meeks said. "The entire train is talking about it. We have the man in custody where he will remain until the next stop."

"Is the victim going to press charges?" Murphy said.

"That's up to him. I just wanted to tell you the railroad is grateful to you for preventing that from turning into a shooting," Meeks said.

"I was just there is all."

"So was everyone else and all they did was watch."

"Mr. Meeks, is it?" Murphy asked. "Do you know about the mass killings out west that shut down the Santa Fe expansion?"

Meeks was taken aback by the question and momentarily at a loss.

"Yes, I do, but how do you?" he finally asked.

Murphy pulled out his billfold and opened it to show his congressional identification.

"You're a congressman from Tennessee?" Meeks asked in amazement.

"That's not for public knowledge," Murphy said. "I'm on a fact-finding expedition to New Mexico to learn about these killings and the shutdown. What can you tell me?"

"Someone is killing workers and the others refuse to work until the man is caught."

"What has the railroad done about it?"

"In catching the man you mean?" Meeks asked. "As far as I know, they have sent out police, set up guards, requested federal aid, and even went to the Army for protection."

"Without results?"

Meeks shook his head. "No, unfortunately, not."

"There must be some ideas as to who is behind the killings and why?"

"I'm sure there is, but I don't know them."

"Well, thank you for your time and please keep this confidential," Murphy said.

"Don't worry, Congressman."

The one that haunted him the most was the church killing. He was the last of the six and hiding in a small Idaho town. A hundred souls in the church were singing a hymn when he opened the doors, walked in, and put a bullet in the back of the raping, murdering bastard's head.

At the sound of the gunshot the congregation was shocked into silence.

Before he walked out, he could see the fear in their eyes.

He looked at them and they lowered their eyes and looked at the floor.

He could smell their sweat and it stank of fear and loathing.

He turned and walked out of the church and no one tried to stop him as he mounted his horse and rode away.

Murphy's eyes snapped open and he looked up at the dark ceiling of his sleeper car. The sheets and pillow were drenched in his own sweat brought on by his nightmare.

He didn't have the nightmare much anymore. Usually it appeared as a premonition of events to come.

Murphy stood up and struck a match to light the oil lamp. He read his pocket watch and it was three in the morning. He filled a tumbler with his father's whiskey and drank half the glass in one long gulp.

The strong Irish whiskey went down like fire.

Murphy coughed, cleared his throat, and took a smaller sip that quieted the burn.

He finished the glass and poured another.

He wanted to sleep but not dream and the sleep he needed was at the bottom of his father's whiskey bottle.

FOUR

An hour before the train arrived in Santa Fe, Murphy went to the last car to groom and brush his horse and then carefully saddled him and slipped on the bridle. When the train stopped and the door opened, the last car was not on the platform and workers slid a ramp into place.

"Come on, Boyle, let's get some sunshine," Murphy said and walked his horse down the ramp to the dirt street.

The platform was swamped with commuters entering and exiting the train. The air was thick with black, foul-smelling smoke. The station was at the end of town and Murphy held the reins and walked Boyle slowly to Main Street.

Nothing much had changed since he last visited Santa Fe except for the string of telegraph poles that ran through town. It was a thriving cowboy town with several corrals and pens at one end and a dozen saloons and brothels on the other.

Murphy walked to the street where the railroad station manager office was located. He tied Boyle to the post outside, then climbed up to the wood sidewalk, opened the door, and entered.

A man was seated at a telegraph desk, tap-tapping away, and didn't look up when Murphy closed the door.

"Excuse me," Murphy said.

"Hold on," the man said.

He continued tapping. When he stopped, he waited for a reply and when it came he wrote it down on paper.

"Is the station . . . ?" Murphy said.

The man ignored Murphy, jumped up from his chair, raced to the door at the end of the room, opened it, and went inside. After a few moments, he rushed back to his desk to start tapping on the telegraph key again.

Murphy walked to him and placed his hand over the telegraph key.

The man looked up. "You can't . . ." he said.

"But I am," Murphy said. "Now, I've asked you twice, or tried to. I'll try again. Is the station manager in the room back there?"

"Yes, but . . ."

Murphy removed his hand, walked to the door, opened it, and stepped inside. A bulky, balding man in a wool suit sat behind a cluttered desk. He looked up from the telegram he was reading.

"Who are you?"

"Are you the station manager?" Murphy said.

"Carl Potts and yes, I am."

Murphy closed the door and walked to the desk.

"How soon can you send a private train out to the site where the workers are on strike?" Murphy said.

"Who the hell are you?" Potts said.

"I work directly for the President," Murphy said and pulled his wallet with his Secret Service identification, hiding his Congress ID, and set it on the desk.

Potts stared at it for a moment. Then his eyes drifted up and focused on Murphy.

"What's happened isn't the fault of the railroad," Potts said. "I can't control the actions of a violent . . ."

"Be quiet, Mr. Potts," Murphy said. "I'm not here looking for blame. Do you think the President would send me out here to play pin the tail on the donkey with you?"

"Then what?" Potts said.

"Find the person or persons responsible

for this mess and put a stop to it. Now how soon can you send that train?"

"Baker?" Potts said, loud enough to be heard through the door.

A moment later the door opened and the telegraph operator stepped inside.

"Do we have a single engine standing by?" Potts asked.

"No, but one is due in tomorrow morning."

"That's all," Potts said.

Baker closed the door.

"That train will take me to the site," Murphy said. "Do you have any railroad police in town?"

"My chief."

Murphy looked at the railroad clock on the wall to the left of the desk.

"Where's a good place to get a steak?" Murphy said.

"The Hotel Santa Fe serves a decent one."

"You and your chief meet me there in thirty minutes, and I'll buy you lunch."

His name was Swan and he had the shifty-eyed appearance of a man who trusted no one, which was exactly the type of man needed for a railroad chief of police.

"I've done all I could to get the men to return to work," Swan said as he cut into his steak. "But after these new killings, they won't budge. The county sheriff reported several more settlers north of the camp have been killed and that doesn't help none."

"Like I told Mr. Potts, I'm not here looking for blame," Murphy said. "Tell me what you've done to protect the workers."

"They refuse to leave camp so I have six armed men patrolling night and day," Swan said. "Most of the men keep to their tents during the day and come out after dark when they think it's safe to move about."

"Is it?"

"Safe?" Swan said. "I wasn't there, but those that were said there was no sign of a shooter anywhere. He had to be a far distance and made two head shots and one to the heart. A man shoots like that no one feels safe in daylight."

"Where are the bodies buried?"

"Brought back here and buried in the cemetery outside of town," Potts said.

"Examined by a doctor first?" Murphy asked.

"What for?" Swan asked. "They were dead before we shipped them back."

"Is there a doctor in town I can talk to?" Murphy said.

"Two, in fact, but why?"

"I like to take notes," Murphy said. He

looked at Swan. "What about the area where the men were shot?"

"What about it?" Swan said.

"Did you section it off?"

"What for? The tracks end, the desert begins, there's nothing there," Swan said.

"What time does that train arrive tomorrow?" Murphy said.

"Ten or thereabouts," Potts said.

"How long a ride to the site?"

"A hundred and twenty miles, about three hours or so."

"It has a car for my horse?"

Potts nodded.

Murphy nodded. "Let's finish our lunch and then see the doctors."

Doctors McCoy and Gertz operated their practice in a large, two-story home at the end of Elm Street where it was secluded for privacy. The home was white with yellow trim and a nice garden of flowers out front.

McCoy was married and lived in a house several blocks away. Gertz, older and a widower, occupied the second floor of the home used as an office.

Both were in when Murphy, Swan, and Potts arrived.

McCoy was in an examination room with a patient. Gertz was writing in a ledger book and drinking tea when his nurse escorted them into the parlor.

"Mr. Potts, Chief Swan, are either of you ill?" Gertz said.

"No, Doctor, but Mr. Murphy would like to ask you a few questions," Potts said.

Gertz looked at Murphy, who towered over Potts and Swan. "Questions?"

"About the three murdered workers from a few weeks ago," Murphy said.

"May I ask who you are?" Gertz asked.

Murphy drew his wallet and flipped it open. Gertz read the identification and nodded. "What about them?"

"Did you examine them prior to their burial?"

"There wasn't much left of the heads of the two who were shot there," Gertz said. "The third had a hole in his chest a melon would fit through."

"Did you recover the bullet or did it pass?"

"It lodged in the spinal cord and I removed it."

"Did you save it?"

Gertz turned and nodded to a pickle jar on a shelf over the fireplace. It was three-quarters' full of bullets.

"Last one on the pile," Gertz said. "No one has been shot since then."

Murphy went to the fireplace and dipped

his hand into the pickle jar and retrieved a distorted, very large bullet, and carried it back to the desk.

Murphy pointed to the lamp "Could you turn that up a bit?"

Gertz enlarged the wick on the lamp.

Murphy held the bullet under the light.

"What the hell is that?" Potts asked.

"A Sharps .50-90 bullet," Murphy said.

"Biggest Goddamn bullet I've ever seen," Potts said.

Murphy looked at Potts. "Buffalo gun," he said.

Swan looked at Murphy. "Are you saying the shooter is a buffalo skinner?"

"I'm saying he used a buffalo gun, a Sharps .50-90 rifle, to kill those men," Murphy said. "That's what I'm saying."

"You sound like you know that weapon," Potts said.

"I do. Doctor, where was the entry wound?"

"Left side a few inches from the heart."

"Thank you, Doctor," Murphy said.

Swan's office was at the far end of the railroad depot. A third the size of Potts's office, it held a desk with two extra chairs, a woodstove, a bulletin board, a locked rifle cabinet, and a small cot where a man could sleep in an emergency.

Swan filled three mugs with coffee from a pot that rested on the woodstove.

"It ain't good, but it's hot," Swan said.

Murphy held the .50-90 bullet up to the light streaking in through the dusty window. "Would you have a magnifying glass I could use?"

"A what? No, I don't," Swan said.

"I believe the women's haberdashery on John Street has one," Potts said. "I've seen them use it to study women's jewelry."

Murphy pocketed the bullet and looked at Swan.

"Mr. Swan, you'll be on the train with me tomorrow," Murphy said.

Swan looked at Murphy.

"I wasn't asking," Murphy said.

Three salesgirls ran the store, but the owner was a man named Duggan. He was a tall Irishman with glasses, a thin crop of fading red hair, and veins in his nose that spoke of whiskey.

"A magnifying glass?" Duggan asked.

Murphy nodded. "Do you have one?"

"Several," Duggan said. "In the office. I use them to study jewelry."

"May I use one for a moment?"

Duggan took Murphy to the office.

"The best one you have," Murphy said.

Duggan opened a desk drawer and removed a large, round magnifying glass and handed it to Murphy.

Murphy dug the bullet out of his pocket, held it to the window, and studied it carefully under the magnifying glass.

"What are you doing?" Duggan said.

"Looking at the grooves in this bullet made by the rifle that fired it."

"Grooves?"

"Markings," Murphy said. "Made by the rifling inside the barrel."

"What for?"

Murphy placed the bullet into his pocket and set the glass on the desk. "Would you have a magnifying glass I could buy?"

"I got more than I use," Duggan said. "You're welcome to have one of them."

In the room he rented at the hotel, Murphy sat at the desk with the lamp on high and studied the .50-90 bullet with the magnifying glass. He opened his notebook and with a pencil he drew the bullet and markings on a page and labeled it *Sharps .50-90 bullet used to kill railroad worker.*

Murphy closed the book and set the lamp to low, removed his shirt and pants, and got under the covers for a quick nap.

He was very familiar with the capabilities of the Sharps rifle. He carried one during the war as a sniper. It was a breechloader capable of one round at a time, but in the hands of an expert ten or more rounds could be fired in one minute.

One shot could bring down a two-thousand-pound buffalo.

In the hands of a skilled shooter the rifle was deadly accurate at twelve hundred yards and even more.

Murphy knew that because he had made just such a shot many times.

He got up for a moment, opened the book, and wrote on the page the word, *Sharpshooter.*

FIVE

The way to build a railroad is with hundreds of men willing to work harder and longer than a pack mule. With thousands of ties and track sections, the tools to dig, lay, and nail, and with buckets of sweat and blood, and sometimes death.

With skilled land surveyors, engineers, carpenters, and planners. With a portable town that could be packed up and moved every ten to twenty miles. In the town would be a general store, saloon, dining hall for the workers, doctor, and a brothel well stocked with women of all shapes, sizes, and races.

Cattle would travel with the town along with several butchers and a hefty supply of vegetables, grains, and whatnot. Cowboys were employed to drive the cattle and see to their care.

When the chief engineer gave the word to move the town it was remarkable how quickly wood and tent structures came apart and were packed away onto flatcars. At the next site chosen by the chief engineer, the town seemingly sprung up within hours.

Murphy had been in railroad towns many times during and after the war and this one was no different than most.

Murphy and Swan were the only passengers on board the two-car train that took them from Santa Fe to the end of the expansion tracks a hundred and twenty or so miles to the northeast.

It had rained all the previous night into early morning and the immediate area around the ten or so buildings was deep-set in mud.

Murphy got Boyle from the last car and, together with Swan, they walked past the temporary buildings to the large tent marked *Railroad Police*.

Swan poked his head through the flaps and then turned to Murphy.

"Empty," he said. "The men must be on patrol."

"Who is the chief engineer?" Murphy asked.

"That would be Mr. Johnson."

"Which is his tent?"

Swan grinned. "He has a private car."

The train of fifteen cars parked on the track ended with two private sleeping cars.

"The last one is his," Swan said as he led Murphy to the car.

"Where are all the men?" Murphy asked as they walked past the major tents and structures of the town.

"In tents sleeping," Swan said. "The brave ones are in the saloon or brothel. It's been this way for weeks."

At the last car in the train, Swan raised his voice, "Mr. Johnson, it's Chief Swan. Are you in there, sir?"

After a few seconds, the door opened and a Chinese man in chef's clothing stepped out to the platform and nodded to Swan.

Swan gestured at the car. "Ah, Mr. Moy, is Mr. Johnson inside?"

Johnson appeared behind Moy.

"Chief Swan," Johnson said. "Is something wrong and who is this man with you?"

"This is Mr. Murphy and he's with Washington," Swan replied.

Johnson looked at Murphy and nodded. "Join me for lunch," he said. "Mr. Moy is a hell of a cook."

■ ■ ■ ■

"Try the chicken dumplings," Johnson said. "They're excellent."

Murphy forked a dumpling from a steaming pile and shoveled it into his mouth. He chewed and washed it down with a sip of Chinese tea.

"Now then, what can I do for you?" Johnson asked.

"You can get these men back to work and finish the Santa Fe Railroad to Dodge City," Murphy said.

"God knows I tried," Johnson said. "Offered double pay and free turns in the brothel but they won't budge until that maniac is caught or killed."

"And how is that going to happen with everyone sitting on their asses in their tents?" Murphy said.

Johnson dumped some rice from a bowl onto his plate, adding some beef and vegetables and a few dumplings. He took a sip of tea and looked at Murphy.

"We've sent out patrols, added extra guards, contacted the Army and US Marshal, and even hired Pinkerton men, and all for naught, Mr. Murphy," Johnson explained. "As long as there is the chance a man's head could be blown off, they won't work. I've threatened to fire them all and hire a new crew, but there isn't a man within five hundred miles who would hire on as long as that lunatic is on the loose, and the men know that. The Dodge City project shut down last week after four men were killed while surveying routes. Did you know that?"

Murphy ate a dumpling. "No."

"I also received word from the county sheriff in Wyoming that a new family of settlers were found murdered on the farmland they purchased," Johnson said. "Husband, wife, and four small children shot and the husband had his throat cut. I'm told the sale of new land has dropped to almost zero. So, let me ask you, Mr. Murphy, what am I supposed to do?"

"Who witnessed the killings on the tracks?" Murphy asked.

"Some of the men," Swan said. "But they didn't see the shooter."

"After lunch let's find them," Murphy said. "Then we'll take a ride to the site."

Johnson raised an eyebrow "Whatever for? There's nothing out there."

Murphy ate a dumpling and took a sip of tea. He looked at Johnson. "Mr. Johnson, I wasn't asking," he said.

■ ■ ■ ■

A hundred or more men were gathered inside the large mess tent where the conversation was an uneasy buzz. The group was a mixture of white, Asian, and black. Most were drinking coffee. A few had shots of whiskey on the side or mixed in with their coffee.

Swan and four of his police entered the tent and the buzz grew louder.

The walking boss, a man named Munro, stood up and looked at Swan. "What's going on, Chief? You caught the man? Is that what this meeting is about?"

Johnson, followed by Murphy, entered the tent.

"Sit down, Mr. Munro," Johnson said.

Munro took his seat.

"This is Mr. Murphy," Johnson said. "He's been sent by Washington to look into our situation and . . ."

"Our situation is some crazy bastard is shooting people for no good reason," Munro said, and the tent went abuzz.

"He has a reason," Murphy said and stared at Munro. "And don't open your mouth again unless I ask you a direct question."

The buzz quieted and all eyes focused on Murphy. In his frock coat he appeared taller and more sinister.

"You men are sitting on your asses while government bonds and private investors are paying for you to do so," Murphy said. "Mr. Munro, who witnessed the shootings?"

"Nobody," Munro said. "Nobody saw the shooter, just his bullets at work."

"But you heard the shots?" Murphy said.

"Me and a few others."

"Are those others in this tent?"

Munro scanned the tent. "Yes."

"You and those others meet at the train in thirty minutes," Murphy said and walked out of the tent.

Dressed in black trail clothes, vest and hat, his gun belt around his waist, Murphy led Boyle to the train where Johnson, Swan, Munro, and three other men waited for him.

Thick black smoke rose from the stack and blew southwest on a breeze.

"She ready to roll?" Murphy asked.

"Whenever you are," Johnson said.

"Let me box my horse and I'll be right with you," Murphy said.

The ride to the end of the line was just short of thirteen miles. A hundred yards of unsecured track lay in front of the two-car train.

The last unsecured rail was covered in dried, black blood.

Murphy looked at the blood, at the splatter patterns, and then said, "Tell me what happened, Mr. Munro."

"What do you mean, what happened?" Munro said. "The men were laying track and shots fired and three men were dead. That's what happened."

"Where were you?"

"Guiding, like I'm supposed to be."

"In front, on the left, where?"

Munro looked at the track. "On the right there."

"The three victims were all on the left?"

Munro nodded. "Yeah."

"How long after the first man fell did you hear the report of the round?" Murphy asked.

"The what?" Munro asked.

"The boom-boom."

Munro shrugged. "I don't know. Two seconds, maybe three."

"That's about right," one of Munro's men said. "Three seconds or so. I saw the second man fall and I jumped on the ground and then I heard the shot."

"You were on the right?" Murphy said.

"The man nodded.

"Put a tier in the air and then count the seconds for my shots," Murphy said.

"What do you mean seconds?" Munro asked.

"The boom-boom."

Murphy retrieved Boyle from the boxcar and rode to the west about eight hundred yards and dismounted on a softly rolling hill of green grass.

He used the binoculars to locate the upright railroad tie. He pulled the Henry rifle from its sleeve and checked the sights. He took careful aim and fired a round into the tie. In open country the shot echoed around him for a moment or two.

Murphy holstered the Henry and rode Boyle a hundred yards up the hill. He adjusted the sights on the Henry and fired a second round.

Then he rode Boyle another hundred yards and fired a third round at the tie.

Having reached the limits of the Henry rifle's capabilities, Murphy rode back to the tracks.

"That's some shooting," Johnson said. "Look at the tie, it's a four-inch spread and from that distance is pretty remarkable."

"Did you count the seconds?" Murphy asked.

"About one on the first," Johnson said. "One and a half on the second. An even two seconds on the third."

Murphy dismounted and looked at the sloping hill in the distance. "I was at a thousand yards," he said. "If Munro is right about three seconds I put him at thirteen hundred yards up there on that hill where a downward shot is easier to make."

Johnson looked at the hill "Thirteen hundred . . . what kind of weapon can make that?"

"A Sharps rifle in the hands of the right man," Murphy said.

"Can you do it?" Swan asked.

"Yes."

Murphy used the binoculars to scan the hill. "I'm going for a quick look."

On the hill Murphy dismounted, tied Boyle to a bush, and scouted the area. The hard rain of the past few days washed away any tracks left by man and horse, but if Murphy was in the mind to kill from a distance unobserved this would be the place.

He walked around a bit looking for some evidence a man had been there, and then he spotted it. A slight incline of soft grass beneath a poplar tree where a few of the low hanging branches had been trimmed.

He got down on his stomach with the binoculars and aimed them at the train and then Johnson's group and finally zeroed in on the upright tie.

Even without a scope the shot was possible.

In his left peripheral vision Murphy caught sight of something and he scanned left and spotted six riders approaching the train. The six stopped and said words with Johnson and Swan. After a few moments the six rode past them and followed the tracks.

Murphy stood up and returned to his horse, mounted up, and rode down to Johnson and the group.

"Looking for work," Johnson said as the two-car train started to move.

Murphy dug out his pipe and tobacco pouch. "What did you tell them?"

Moy served coffee from a silver carafe into fine china cups with saucers.

"I've lost fifty men," Johnson said. "They said they worked the A&P, the Southern Pacific, and the Pennsylvania out of Philly. I told them to wait for me and if they could hold on until we get these men back to work I'd hire them on."

Murphy stuffed his pipe, struck a match, and looked out the window at the scenery rolling by. Then he looked at Swan. "Any of the men armed?"

"Just my police. Why?"

"Men feel more apt to come out of the dark when they can defend themselves."

Johnson nodded. "You mean arm the men and they might agree to work?"

"Unarmed men in this country might as well be naked men," Murphy said. "Even if you armed, say, two dozen men to stand watch that's still a lot better than the entire lot sitting on their asses getting fat."

Johnson looked at Swan. "What do we have locked up?"

"Three dozen Winchester 75's and the like amount in Colt revolvers and ammo for both in numbers," Swan said.

"Pick two dozen qualified men and arm them," Johnson said. "Along with your six that should be more than enough to get the men working again."

Murphy looked out the window and puffed on his pipe. "How close can the railroad get me to Dodge City?"

"If you ride east and north the closest would be Wichita," Johnson said.

Murphy picked up his coffee and took a sip. He nodded his approval at Moy.

As the train rolled to a slow stop a hundred

66

yards from the encampment, gunshots were heard over the loud steam engine.

Murphy looked at Johnson. "Do you pay the men in cash?"

"I do because . . . someone is shooting."

Swan went to the window, lowered it, and peered out.

"How much is on hand and where?" Murphy asked.

"Thirty-seven thousand dollars in cash and in the safe in the paymaster's tent," Johnson said.

"Swan, you're armed, you come with me," Murphy said.

Johnson went to the window. "What's going on?"

"Those cowboys looking for a job you sent here, it appears the job they came for was to rob your safe," Murphy said. "Let's go, Mr. Swan."

Swan looked at Murphy.

"I wasn't asking," Murphy said.

Murphy slid the rear door of the car open and jumped down, pulling his Schofield .45 in the process.

He looked at the center of the encampment. Two of Swan's police lay dead in the street outside the paymaster's tent. The six cowboys were rolling the heavy safe on a trolley cart from the tent to their waiting horses.

Murphy cocked the .45 as he walked toward them. At a distance of fifty feet, one of them noticed Murphy and went for his Colt. Murphy shot him in the head.

Immediately the five men released the safe and drew their weapons and Murphy shot a second and then a third in less than three seconds.

The remaining three ran for cover beside the boxcar of the two-car train Murphy had ridden on from Santa Fe, and Murphy shot a fourth in the back before the other two ducked behind the car.

"Give it up and I'll allow you to live," Murphy said as he took cover behind the locomotive of the two-car train.

"Screw you," one of them said and opened fire at Murphy.

Murphy fired the remaining two shots in the .45 and then opened the top to automatically eject the spent shells. As he dipped into a pocket for fresh shells to reload, Swan ran up beside him.

"You killed them before I could jump down," he said. "Where are the others?"

"Behind the boxcar," Murphy said as he fed the Schofield.

"How many?"

"Two."

Reloaded, Murphy closed the top and cocked the hammer.

"Listen up you two," he said. "We have your horses and can arm thirty-six men with Winchesters so toss out your guns and we won't kill you. Otherwise I'll kill you both right now."

"Can we ride out of here?" one of them asked.

"Of course you can't," Murphy said. "Don't be stupid."

"Then we'll take our chances," one of them said.

Murphy waved to Swan to go around the boxcar.

"What chance?" Murphy said. "You have no chance but to give up."

Swan went down the side of the long boxcar, pressed his body against the side, and looked back at Murphy.

"You have sixty seconds to give up," Murphy said. "After then it's too late."

"I guess it's too late then," one of them said. "Start counting."

Murphy walked down the side of the boxcar and stood beside Swan. Murphy nodded to Swan and then stepped around and shot the man closest to him, who was on his knees.

The last man spun around as Murphy hit him in the face with the barrel of the Schofield, knocking him unconscious.

When the last man opened his eyes, he was seated in a hard chair inside a tent. Murphy, Swan, and Johnson were standing in front of him with cups of coffee.

Murphy stepped forward. "What's your name?"

"Why should I tell you shit?"

"Because if you don't I'll shoot you in the balls."

"No man would do that to another man."

Murphy pulled the .45, cocked it, and took aim.

"Kent. Andrew Kent."

Murphy nodded, de-cocked the .45, and holstered it.

"So, Kent, tell me, what was this all about?" Murphy asked.

"What do you mean about?"

"The robbery, what did you think?"

"What are you going to do with me?"

"Take you back to Santa Fe and give you to the sheriff."

"Then why should I tell you anything more?"

"Because if you don't I'll hang you right now for murder and have myself a steak right after."

Kent stared at Murphy and then slowly nodded his head.

"Me and the others worked laying track out of Dodge," Kent said. "After the men shut it down, refusing to work, me and my friends were drinking in the saloon and met a bunch from here who quit for the same reason. We got to talking about all the money sitting in the safe here and in the Dodge camp and how easy it would be to take seeing as how nobody but the railroad police are armed. We switched places. We came here and they went there figuring no one would recognize us. We didn't count on a son of a bitch like you being around."

"So men from this camp plan to rob the safe from the Dodge camp," Murphy said.

"By now they either got away clean or they're dead," Kent said. "Unless they got another one like you over there, they got away clean is my guess."

"Well, you didn't," Murphy said. "Swan, watch him."

Murphy and Johnson went outside the tent.

"Get your train fired up," Murphy said. "We have to send a telegram from Santa Fe to Dodge."

Along with the sheriff in Santa Fe, Murphy and Johnson stood in the telegraph office while the operator wrote the reply to Murphy's telegraph on a slip of paper.

"Read it," Murphy said when the operator stopped writing.

"Seven men robbed the safe at the Dodge railroad camp," the operator said. "Forty thousand dollars. Two were killed, the other five got away. The sheriff in Dodge formed a posse. Three railroad police, the walking boss, and paymaster were killed during the robbery."

"Mr. Johnson, how far by horse to the Dodge City railroad camp?" Murphy asked.

"Five days of hard riding," Johnson replied.

"I'll stay the night in town and leave from your camp in the morning."

"You're welcome to use my sleeper car," Johnson said.

"Thanks, but no."

"Join me for dinner at least?"

"What's Moy cooking?"

Six

Murphy stood before the railroad workers in the crowded mess hall tent and quietly sipped coffee from a tin cup.

Johnson and Swan stood to Murphy's left.

"Mr. Johnson and Mr. Swan will arm twenty-four men with Winchester rifles and sidearms for the sole purpose of protecting the rest of you men while you resume work," Murphy said. "Any man that doesn't want to work can pack his gear and the train will take you back to Santa Fe. You'll draw whatever pay you have coming, but you lose your signing bonus. It's up to you, but one way or another, this line will get built."

Munro stood up. "After what we seen you did yesterday, we'll work," he said. "All of us."

Johnson stepped forward. "Then let's get to it."

With Boyle loaded with enough supplies to

last until he reached the Dodge railroad camp, Murphy stood in front of the train and shook hands with Johnson and Swan.

"Think that sheriff will catch those boys?" Johnson asked.

"No," Murphy said.

"Are you coming back this way?"

"Only if the evidence tells me to."

"Mind me asking what someone like you is doing in Washington?" Johnson asked.

"Mostly hiding from myself," Murphy said.

Murphy mounted Boyle, touched a finger to his hat, and rode northeast toward Dodge City.

Bacon sizzled in a large skillet over the campfire. Murphy added an ounce of his father's whiskey to the pan for flavor. In another pan he laid out two cups of beans with water to boil. He removed two biscuits from wax paper and ate them while he waited.

He had covered twenty miles today and aimed for more than that tomorrow if Boyle was willing. He wanted to reach the Dodge railroad camp inside of four days. It was possible one of the workers saw something. He wanted to check the bullets used to kill the victims, although he had no doubt they would be .50-90 Sharps round.

When the bacon and beans were ready, he dumped them both onto a tin plate and ate two more biscuits with it and some hot coffee.

Afterward, he checked on Boyle and then extinguished the fire and got into his bedroll.

Thirty-six hours and nearly forty-five miles later, Murphy spotted a flock of buzzards circling about a half mile in the distance.

However many were in the air he knew a like amount would be on the ground. He rode toward the buzzards in no hurry, allowing Boyle a breather.

Around five hundred yards from the circling buzzards, he spotted a large group of them on the ground. They were picking at carcasses, jumping and jockeying for position. Murphy drew out the Winchester, aimed carefully, and shot a buzzard in its chest. The other birds scattered and some took flight.

Holding the Winchester in his left hand, Murphy said, "I'm not liking this, Boyle. Let's go see what those bastards were picking at."

Riding slowly to the buzzards, Boyle snorted nervously and Murphy had to calm him by rubbing his neck.

"Okay, I'll get off here, but don't you run off," Murphy said as he dismounted.

He removed leather strips from a saddlebag and hobbled Boyle a hundred yards from the buzzards, then gave him some sugar cubes.

"Behave yourself," Murphy said. "I won't be long."

Walking toward the buzzards, he cocked the lever of the Winchester and shot another bird dead, reloaded, and shot another.

The flock scattered, landed a safe distance away, and waited.

Murphy walked into four dead men in a tight-knit group and a fifth ten or so yards away. The fifth dead man wore the sheriff's badge from Dodge City.

"Shit," Murphy said aloud.

The buzzards went for the eyes first; they always do, and pecked them clean out of the five dead men. Next they went for the open wounds where a bullet had torn large holes in all five men. They did a good job ripping open and tearing out flesh.

Murphy scanned the horizon in all directions and there was no sign of the dead men's horses. They were probably miles away. He knelt beside the sheriff. The man was about forty or so, rugged-looking in life, frightened in death from the frozen expression of fear on his face. The buzzards had pecked out his eyes so Murphy couldn't tell what color they were.

Murphy drew the large knife from its sheath on the left side of his holster. He used the sharp tip to dig into the gaping hole in the sheriff's stomach and dug around until he found the bullet that was lodged against the spine and dug it out. Even flattened and covered in dried blood he could see it was a Sharps .50-90 slug.

Murphy pocketed the slug and then caught sight of the buzzards a hundred feet or so to the right behind some brush. They had gathered around a sixth body and were squawking and fighting over the flesh.

He drew the Schofield and fired two shots at the buzzards and they scattered. He walked to the sixth body and stood over him. There was a large hole in his chest and something extra.

His throat was cut nearly ear to ear.

Somehow he survived the bullet to his chest and . . .

Murphy traced the tracks from his horse.

And he rode to this point before falling off his horse.

The shooter saw him fall and came to investigate, found him still alive, came up behind him, and finished him off with the knife.

Murphy knelt down and inspected the cut. It sliced right to left.

The shooter was left-handed.

Murphy knelt and felt the man's fingers and under the knife cut in the neck. Rigor mortis had set in maybe twelve hours ago. The man was dead at least fifteen.

He stood and inspected the terrain. There were a hundred places to set up an ambush in the rolling hills, trees, and grass, especially if you could pick off your victims from twelve hundred or more yards away.

There was no sign of the forty thousand stolen from the Dodge railroad camp.

Murphy stood over the stacked bodies and poured some of his father's whiskey onto the tumbleweeds he had gathered to cover the bodies with. He removed their gun belts, cash, and the sheriff's badge and stored them with his gear. He struck a match and set fire to the tumbleweeds. Within seconds the weeds were engulfed in flames and spread quickly to the clothes and then flesh.

The stench of melting fat and burning flesh was overpowering and Murphy backed away and returned to Boyle.

The buzzards were circling high in the air.

"Sorry fellows, this restaurant is closed," Murphy said.

Around a campfire, as bacon, beans, and coffee cooked, Murphy ate a few sticks of jerked beef and dug out his notebook and pencil. He made a note.

Shooter is left-handed.

He rinsed off the slug taken from the dead body earlier and used the magnifying glass to inspect it carefully by the light of the campfire.

He dug out the first .50-90 slug and placed both slugs side by side in the palm of his right hand as he held the magnifying glass over them. Although the slugs were damaged on impact, the markings and grooves on them were identical.

He made a note.

Men from Santa Fe camp and a likely posse were killed by same .50-90 Sharps rifle.

"A left-handed sharpshooter," Murphy said aloud. "About as hard to find as a one-legged can-can dancer."

Six men armed with Winchester rifles greeted Murphy when he rode into the Dodge City railroad camp.

"Are you Murphy?" one of them asked.

"I am," Murphy said.

"We got a telegram from Santa Fe said you were coming," the man said. "I'll walk you over to see Mr. Bradley."

The Dodge camp was a mirror image of the camp in Santa Fe. Murphy met Thomas Bradley in his private car at the end of the twenty-car train.

"My counterpart tells me they resumed working," Bradley said.

"Johnson and Swan have their men back at work, yes," Murphy said. "Only because they agreed to arm twenty-four men with Winchesters and have them on patrol the entire time."

Bradley nodded. "I'm sure I can persuade the men to return to work under a similar plan."

"Good, now I have some questions," Murphy said. "So I might as well start with you. Were there any witnesses to the shootings that stopped production, by you or anyone else?"

"I happened to be in my car working on plans for a bridge when the first shootings took place," Bradley said.

"Do you have a police chief?"

"That position happens to be vacant at the moment."

"Can you assemble everyone in camp in

the mess tent in one hour?"

"All right."

"Now, what can you tell me about the robbery?"

"Seven heavily armed men rode in shooting up the place, grabbed the paymaster, and forced him to open the safe," Bradley said. "They killed five of my people, but the police got two of them in the process. They made off with forty thousand dollars in a satchel."

"Did you know the sheriff was killed along with five others on the plains between here and Santa Fe?"

"No, but that explains why he didn't return," Bradley said. "He sent most of the posse back after two days and continued on with just the four, I guess, because he told them he was going to meet up with a federal marshal in Lamar."

"The same man who killed the Santa Fe workers and yours killed them."

"How do you know?"

"I dug a .50-90 Sharps round out of a victim in Santa Fe and one out of the sheriff on the plains."

"Jesus Christ. It doesn't make sense," Bradley said. "None of this makes sense. What about the men who robbed the money?"

"No sign of them. The shooter probably arrived after they passed through, or maybe he killed them at another location."

"The money's a big loss to be sure, but the home office will have to replace it," Bradley said.

"The bodies of the victims are where?"

"Sent to Dodge," Bradley said. "By now in the cemetery."

"You have a place to take a bath around here? I could use one."

"Sally Orr runs the whores," Bradley said. "She has six tubs from back east behind her tent for the workers to clean up first before they take a turn."

"Make the meeting in an hour and a half," Murphy said. "I got a lot of trail soreness to soak out."

Sally Orr ran the brothel and employed twelve girls and two men as bodyguards. She had a dozen small tents with cots and six bathtubs behind her main tent where men made their selections.

Sally was a buxom blonde woman of about thirty-five or so and acted as greeter and screener for each male who entered her tent.

"You're a tall one," Sally said when Murphy entered the tent. "Lucy is my tallest girl if you . . ."

"All I want is a hot bath and a bar of soap," Murphy said.

Sally took a closer look at Murphy, took in the custom-made Schofield on his right hip and the black trail clothes, and knew immediately that this man was used to giving orders and not taking them.

"Behind the tent," Sally said. "I have hot water boiling. I'll fill a tub while you strip down. Do you want your clothes washed?"

"How long?"

"Fifteen minutes to wash, about an hour to air-dry in front of a fire. Cost you two bucks on top of the two for the bath."

"Okay."

"Would you care for a drink while they fill the tub?"

"You have coffee?"

"I do."

"How much is that?"

Sally took Murphy's arm and had to tilt her head back to look up at him and smile. "Coffee's on the house."

Murphy sat in the tub of hot water up to his neck. His lit pipe dangled from his lips and he made a deep sigh as he puffed.

Beside the tub a bar of soap, towels, scrub brush, and a fresh mug of coffee rested on a small table.

He reached for the coffee and took a sip.

The weariness in his bones and muscles started to slowly fade as the hot water worked its magic. Hard riding was easier a decade ago, but so was everything else.

"So, cowboy, would you like a shave and a haircut?" Sally said from behind him.

"Are you also a barber?" Murphy said.

"And a damn good one," Sally said. "All the men get shaved and clipped from me instead of in Dodge."

Sally walked to the tub and took the chair beside it.

Murphy sipped coffee and looked at her. Then he scratched his beard. "I suppose my beard could use some grooming."

"Your hair, too. It's long enough for a ponytail."

"All right. I won't be long."

"Cowboy, just dunk down and get your hair wet," Sally said. "I'll take it from there."

Murphy looked at her.

"Oh, honey, I've seen them all many times before," Sally said. "There's no reason to be shy."

Murphy set the mug and his pipe on the table.

"I'll get my bag," Sally said and stood up.

Murphy dunked under the water, came

up, and slicked his hair back with his hand.

Sally returned with a small satchel, the kind a doctor would carry. She set it on the table and removed a comb and scissors.

She stood directly behind Murphy and ran the comb through his wet hair.

"Not too much," Murphy said.

"Just relax," Sally said and started to snip at his hair.

Murphy grabbed his pipe and coffee.

"Everybody in camp is talking about you," Sally said. "About how you killed those men who robbed the Santa Fe payroll and got the men back to work."

"It isn't that difficult to kill amateurs," Murphy said. "And the men were ready to go back to work. They just needed a little reassurance and a slight push."

Sally ran the comb through Murphy's hair and snipped. Little bunches of hair fell into the tub.

"People are saying you're some kind of government man," Sally said. "Is that true?"

"People talk too much and don't say a great deal worth listening to while they're doing it," Murphy said.

Sally set the scissors on the table and ran the comb through Murphy's hair. "Much better," she said. "Dunk under again to rinse."

Murphy dunked under, counted to ten, and surfaced.

Sally held a straight razor and shaving soap in her hands. "I'm going to take a little off your neck and then trim down that bird's nest on your face."

"Not too close," Murphy cautioned.

Sally dipped the soap into the water and worked up a lather and then spread it along Murphy's neck.

"Now hold still," she said. "And tilt your head back."

Murphy titled his head back and Sally carefully scraped his neck clean. She rinsed the razor and picked up the scissors.

"Look at me," Sally said and moved the chair so she could sit closer to the tub.

Murphy turned and looked at Sally.

Sally ran the comb through Murphy's beard and snipped it close with the scissors.

"So, cowboy, I'm of a mind to strip down and join you in that tub," Sally said. "And that's something I never offer."

"Don't," Murphy said.

Sally paused and looked at him.

"My wife wouldn't approve," Murphy said.

Sally nodded and continued snipping. "I respect that," she said. "You have to be the only man in the entire territory who would stay true to his wife. Where is she?"

"Buried with my child in Tennessee," Murphy said.

Sally lowered the scissors. "I'm sorry."

"Don't be," Murphy said. "It was a long time ago."

Sally nodded. "I'll see if your clothes are dry."

Bradley addressed the men inside the mess hall tent. Murphy stood quietly in the background and listened.

Gathered outside the tent, Sally and her girls stood and watched.

After speaking for some time, Bradley concluded with, "There you have it men. Let's put it to a vote. All in favor of returning to work under armed protection raise your hands."

Ninety percent raised their hands.

"Okay, I need a new walking boss and chief of police," Bradley said. "Tom, you were second boss so you're it. I'll select a new chief later. Right now Mr. Murphy has a few questions."

Murphy walked forward and stood beside Bradley.

"Who witnessed the killings?" Murphy asked. "Closest to them, I mean."

Five men held up their hands.

"Can any of you five tell me how long it took from when the bullets struck before you heard the report of the rounds?" Murphy said.

The five men stared at Murphy.

"The gunshots," Murphy said.

"You mean in seconds?" one of the five asked.

"Exactly."

"Three seconds, maybe closer to four."

"You other four agree?" Murphy said.

The four men nodded.

"Thank you," Murphy said.

The ride to the last rails laid by the men took thirty-five minutes by Bradley's private car.

Murphy walked the rails to the end where they were splattered with dried blood.

Bradley stood beside him. "What are you looking at?"

Murphy held up his right hand to Bradley as he studied the blowback pattern on the rails. He turned and scanned the terrain. Looming hills were to the west. Flat land was to the right.

"Those hills, that's where he was when he shot your men," Murphy said.

Bradley looked at the hills in disbelief. "That's three, maybe four hundred yards away at least."

"It will be dark soon," Murphy said. "I don't have time to ride over and take a look. Can you put me up for the night and I'll check in the morning."

"My car has an extra bedroom," Bradley said.

"A tent will be fine."

"Will you at least join me for dinner? My chef is excellent."

"Sure," Murphy said as he stared at the hills.

"This is William Jefferson Parker and he was born a slave in 1830," Bradley said. "He was trained as house chef for the Parker Plantation in Georgia. After the war he migrated to Boston and attended culinary. He's been with me twelve years and I wouldn't let him go for all the tea in China."

Murphy looked at Parker. The man's skin was the color of coffee. His eyes were bright brown. The top of his head was bald, but the crown of hair that surrounded his head was snow white and thick.

"Baked chicken and strips of beef with potatoes, carrots, and corn," Parker said. "Would you care for a drink before I serve?"

"Two snifters of brandy should do," Bradley said.

"Very good," Parker said and left the dining room.

"William travels with me on business and lives with my family when I'm home," Bradley said. "Oh, hell, I shouldn't say lives with my family, he is part of my family."

Murphy looked at the third place setting.

"And always takes his meals with me," Bradley said.

Parker returned with two snifters of brandy. "Thirty minutes to dinner," he said.

"Thank you, William," Bradley said.

Murphy sampled the brandy.

"Do you think it's possible this madman could be an ex-employee of the railroad?" Bradley asked.

"No, I don't," Murphy said.

"Reason?"

"Any man who can shoot and kill like him wouldn't be laying ties for the railroad."

Bradley nodded.

"And that doesn't explain the settlers," Murphy said.

"No, I guess it doesn't."

Parker's culinary skills lived up to Bradley's high praise. Dinner was as good as or better than any restaurant Murphy visited in New York, Boston, San Francisco, or Washington. Dessert was custard served warm with fresh whipped cream and coffee.

"I'm surprised you don't weigh three hundred pounds," Murphy told Bradley.

"Breakfast is always light as is lunch," Parker said. "Tell me, will you be returning to the trail?"

"Yes."

"Would you like some corn dodgers for the trip?" Parker suggested. "I can whip up two hundred in no time."

"Two hundred?"

"They're quite good," Bradley said. "William makes them for the men several times a week to take to the field."

"You got yourself a deal, William," Murphy said. "And now I think I'll turn in. I'd like to return to the site by sunrise."

"William can have one of his light breakfasts for us on the trip," Bradley said.

"Goodnight then," Murphy said.

Murphy walked from the train at the edge of camp to the main section of buildings. It was dark and a dozen or more oil lamps suspended on poles lit the way. He walked past the large tent that housed the saloon, and laughter and piano music filtered outside.

He continued walking to the last tent, Sally Orr's tent, and heard soft whispers and laughter from behind closed flaps. He turned right and walked to the open field where fifty or more two-room tents were pitched.

Suspended oil lamps lit the way and he located a two-man tent that had his name written on a wood sign out front.

Light from an oil lamp illuminated the interior of the tent.

Murphy opened a flap and stepped inside.

Sally was under the covers of a large cot.

She looked at him.

Murphy looked at her.

"I know what you told me, but your wife is dead and you're not," Sally said. "And no amount of self-suffering is going to bring her back or ease your pain. Only living will. I may not know much, but I know that."

Murphy closed the tent flap.

"All I want is to get some sleep," he said.

Sally patted the cot. "Then come get some sleep," she said. "If you wake up during the night and decide you want a little something else you won't have far to go to find it."

Murphy stared at her.

Sally patted the cot again.

Murphy slowly removed his jacket and gun belt and hung them over a chair.

"Do you snore?" he said.

"Of course not. Do you?"

"No."

"Then let's have a nightcap and toast to peace and quiet."

Seven

Murphy and Bradley ate a light breakfast on the ride to the end of the line. They drank coffee and watched the sun slowly rise over the hills from the platform. When the hills glowed bright yellow, Murphy stepped down and, followed by Bradley, walked to the boxcar for his horse.

Bradley rode a large pinto. He didn't carry a sidearm, but a Winchester rifle was slung in a sheath on his saddle.

Murphy led the way to the hills with Bradley at his left.

Parker watched from the platform as they rode away.

As they neared the hills, Bradley said, "Exactly what do you hope to find?"

"Don't know," Murphy said. "Maybe nothing, maybe something."

They rode up the hill and when it leveled off they dismounted.

Murphy took his binoculars and they

started walking along the plateau.

Bradley inspected the ground as they walked. "What are you looking for?"

"I found it," Murphy said.

On the flat plateau beside a tree, branches had been cleared away for a clear line of sight. Directly behind the tree were the remains of a campfire. Murphy knelt before the remains and stirred the ashes with a twig.

"He camped out?" Bradley said with some surprise in his voice.

Murphy nodded. "He waited for your men to reach this spot. From the ashes I'd say three days. How much track can they put down in three days?"

"A full crew of two hundred can make three miles in that time."

Murphy used the binoculars to scan to his left. The tracks curved slightly around a bend and disappeared. He lowered the binoculars and turned around. Behind him the hills gently rolled down to open country.

"He wanted the best place for a clear shot and this is it," Murphy said. "With an easy back door."

"He stalked us."

"That's right."

"That means . . . that means the killings aren't random as believed, but planned."

"That's also right."

Murphy scanned the area around the tree where the shooter stalked his victims.

Bradley looked in the distance at the end of the train tracks. "That's a hell of a shot."

"Fourteen hundred yards is my guess," Murphy said.

Bradley turned and was about to take a step toward his pinto when Murphy yelled, "Stop!"

Bradley froze in place. "What is it?"

Murphy picked up a twig, knelt down, and inserted it into a spent .50-90 Sharps rifle cartridge. He stood and showed it to Bradley.

"Good God, you could bring down a buffalo with that," Bradley said.

"That's what it was designed to do. Let's go."

On the ride back to camp, Parker served coffee with cookies right out of the oven.

"Do you have writing paper and pencil?" Murphy asked Parker.

"In the desk, William," Bradley said.

Parker went to the desk and returned with a stack of paper and several pencils.

Murphy separated the stack into two piles and then removed the .50-90 Sharps cartridge from his vest pocket and placed it on one stack. From his pants pocket he removed a small pen knife and drew out the blade.

With the pen knife Murphy whittled the wood casing off the pencil until a two-inch section of the graphite in the middle was exposed. Then he held the graphite over the Sharps cartridge and slowly whittled it until the cartridge was coated in black dust.

"What are you doing?" Bradley asked.

"Most people think pencils contain lead sticks in the middle, but they don't," Murphy said. "The stick is made of graphite, but centuries ago they believed it was a form of lead, but it isn't."

When the .50-90 cartridge was completely covered in dust, Murphy set the knife and pencil aside, picked up another pencil, and inserted it into the cartridge. Gently rolling the cartridge over the paper flattened the dust tightly against the metal until it was black.

Murphy held the pencil up and looked at the cartridge.

"Mr. Parker, would you blow on the cartridge please?" Murphy said.

Parker leaned in close and blew and as he did Murphy spun the pencil until most of the dust was removed.

"That's good," Murphy said.

"I still don't understand what you're do-ing," Bradley said.

"See that black stain on the metal?" Mur-phy said. "Those lines and grooves?"

"Yes."

"Mr. Parker?"

"I see it, too."

"That is an impression of his thumb," Murphy said. "A print if you will and unique to him and no one else on earth."

Bradley and Parker stared at the thumb print.

"You mean that mark belongs to our shooter?" Bradley asked.

"It does," Murphy said.

"We all have marks like that?" Bradley said and looked at his fingers.

"Yes and unique to anyone else," Murphy said. "And you leave them on every surface you touch even if you can't see them."

"I've seen them when I've washed glasses and the windows," Parker said.

"Exactly right," Murphy said.

The train started to slow its speed and Murphy said, "How long before your train can take me to Dodge?"

"We'll take my private car," Bradley said. "About an hour."

Murphy took coffee in the mess tent while

he waited for the train to be loaded with water and coal and for the wheels and gears to be greased.

There were few others inside the giant tent as work had resumed in the morning and most of the men were out laying track.

As he stuffed his pipe Sally came up behind him and said, "Need a light, cowboy?"

Murphy had a match in his hand, struck it on the table, and lit the pipe.

"Well, then how about a refill?" Sally smiled.

She took the chair opposite Murphy and waved at the man behind the serving counter. He carried a pot and extra cup to the table, touched up Murphy's mug, and filled Sally's.

"Thanks, Sam," Sally said.

Murphy lifted his mug and sipped, set it down, and blew smoke from his pipe.

"I woke up and you were gone," Sally said.

"I told you I had to leave early," Murphy said.

"And now?"

"I'm going to Dodge as soon as the train is ready."

"Coming back?"

"Just to get my horse."

Sally sipped coffee and stared at Murphy

for a moment. "Tell me something, cowboy, is it me? Am I too old for your taste or is it I'm just not attractive to you? Would you prefer the company of one of my younger girls or maybe you just don't like whores?"

"I thought you were the madam?" Murphy said.

Sally reached into the pocket of her long skirt and removed a thin cigar and a match. She struck the match and lit the cigar and blew a smoke ring.

"I acquired a taste for these in Saint Louis a few years back," she said. "I run a house in the north end and all the fashionable ladies smoke these. In private, of course. No self-respecting woman would be seen smoking in public, or taking a drink for that matter."

"Is that where you're from?"

Sally shook her head. "Back east. New Jersey, but my parents came west when I was seven. They died of cholera when I was nine."

"How did you . . . ?"

"Become a madam?"

"Survive?"

"Oh. Well, this was when gold fever hit almost everybody in the country," Sally said. "My parents included. They died in Colorado and I stayed in the miner's camp for two years or so. Families took care of me, fed me, and made sure I had clothes. The camp dried up when I was eleven. Mrs. Orr took me in and I traveled to Saint Louis with her and her family of ten girls."

"Whores?"

"Of course, whores. What did you think? Preachers?"

"That's where you took the name from?"

Sally nodded. "Mrs. Orr kept me separated from her business until I was sixteen," she said. "She made sure I had a proper education and when she felt I was old enough she taught me how to be a madam. When I was eighteen I was running her place. When she died I took her name and her business."

"How did you come to be here with the railroad?"

"A railroad gets built on three basic things," Sally said. "Men willing to work until they drop. Unlimited access to whiskey. And women. When the railroad announced they were extending the Santa Fe they secretly recruited a madam to handle the women. That would be me. The money flows like water. I hired a woman to run my business in Saint Louis while I conduct business here."

"So you'll go back to Saint Louis once

the Santa Fe is completed?"

"Yes."

From outside the mess tent a whistle blew several times.

"That's for me," Murphy said.

"Come say goodbye when you get back from Dodge."

Murphy nodded as he stood up from the table.

As he sat at the dining table in Bradley's private car, Murphy studied the .50-90 shell casing he had retrieved from the hill. The thumb print was still visible and he used the magnifying glass to inspect the grooves and wavy lines left on the metal.

Judging from the print the man's thumb was large, larger than Murphy's own. If his other fingers were proportionate to the thumb he had enormous hands. To handle a Sharps the way that he did required great strength. If his body was in line with his hands the shooter was a big fellow.

Bigger than Murphy and he was considered giant in physical status.

He opened his notebook and made a notation.

How does a giant hide in plain sight?

Murphy lifted the delicate coffee cup off the table and took a sip. He set the cup down and scribbled another note.

Answer. No one knows who he is so no one knows he's a giant.

Murphy closed the notebook and took it and the coffee to the seats beside the window. The countryside rolled by at forty miles an hour, a dizzying speed. He sipped and looked out the window until the cup was empty and then sat back and closed his eyes.

The scent of Sally's hair was still in his nostrils. It smelled of sweet flowers and lemon. He didn't realize it when he slipped under the covers that she was naked and the heat from her body was like standing next to a burning woodstove. He kept his distance as did she, but sometime during the night she rolled over and he awoke feeling her warm flesh pressed against his back.

He listened to her soft breathing and felt her breath on his neck.

It stirred memories of his wife and he forced his mind to shut down and go blank.

He fell back asleep and awoke ninety minutes before dawn. Sally had rolled over again and her face was pressed against his chest and her right leg was draped over him.

Her scent was strong, nearly overpowering. He felt forgotten heat in his loins begin to awaken and he gently untangled himself from her and stood up from the cot. He dressed quickly, quietly, and left her sleeping in the cot and went to the mess tent for coffee.

Murphy opened his eyes and pulled out his watch.

He should be in Dodge inside the hour.

He closed his eyes and took a nap.

Holding a small satchel, Murphy stepped off the train and was greeted by the engineer.

"Will you be making the return trip tonight or in the morning?" the engineer asked.

"Tomorrow. How soon can you be here?"

"Noon."

"All right," Murphy said.

As the engineer returned to the train, Murphy walked from the depot at the edge of town to Main Street.

Dodge City had grown quite a bit since he last visited in '74. The streets were wood and elevated a foot high with steps at every crossing. While most buildings were constructed of wood he noticed several newer buildings constructed of red brick.

The sheriff's office was on Main Street, but the marshal's office was on the opposite end of town on Oak Street.

He walked to Oak Street.

Murphy stood in front of the marshal's office for a moment and took in the streets. The growth came from cattle drives. Dodge was an attractive stopover for weary cowboys on the range.

He counted five hotels and ten saloons just in the short walk from the train depot to Oak Street.

Cowboys on a drive needed a saloon to drink in and a hotel room to sleep it off in and there was no shortage of saloon girls to keep them company in-between.

Murphy opened the door and entered the marshal's office. The marshal was behind his desk.

"What can I do for you?" he asked.

"Are you Marshal Poule?"

"I am."

Murphy removed his wallet and held his identification up for Poule to look at.

"Bradley wired me you were coming," Poule said. "Want some coffee? I just made it."

"Sure."

Murphy walked to the woodstove in the corner of the office where a coffee pot rested and picked it up and a tin mug from the table beside it and filled the mug and returned to the desk.

"Bradley tells me you got his men and the Santa Fe crew back to work," Poule said.

"They were ready, anyway," Murphy said. "The victims of the shooter, were they examined by a doctor before they were buried?"

"Doc Adams checked them before they went to the undertaker."

"I'd like to talk to him."

"I'll walk you over to his office."

"The sheriff is dead you know."

"I know. There's an election next Tuesday to pick a new one."

"Were you with the posse where the sheriff was killed?"

"No. I was in Kansas City on a federal matter."

"It was ugly."

Poule nodded and then stood up. "So is everything else when it comes to slaughtering innocent men, women, and children."

Doctor Adams set up shop twenty years ago on the second floor of a wood building at the end of Elm Street away from the saloons and hotels. His office had three examination rooms, a waiting room, and his office.

"Doc, this is Mr. Murphy from Washington," Poule said.

Behind his desk, Adams removed his

eyeglasses and looked at Murphy.

"He has some questions," Poule said.

Adams was a tiny man, sixty years old with gray hair and blue eyes.

"Questions?" Adams said. "About what?"

"About the men who were shot on the railroad," Murphy said. "Did you examine them and remove the bullets?"

"I did. Why?"

"Did you keep the bullets?"

"I did. I always do when I remove one from a man, dead or alive."

"May I have them?"

"What for?"

"Evidence."

Poule nodded to Adams and the doctor stood up and crossed the room to a tall chest and opened the top door.

"Over here," he said.

Murphy walked to the chest and Adams handed him a large tin can. Murphy removed the lid and looked into the can at the more than five hundred bullets inside.

Murphy shook his head. "You're kidding me?"

"Actually, I am," Adams said. "The marshal told me yesterday you'd be coming around. I figured you'd want to see the bullets. I got them right here."

Adams lifted a glass jar and handed it to

Murphy.

"Six bullets from five victims," Adams said.

Murphy removed the lid and spilled the bullets onto the desk. "Five victims?"

"One was shot twice."

Murphy spread the slugs with his fingers. Five were .50-90 Sharps bullets. The sixth was a Smith & Wesson .44 slug he recognized as belonging to the .44 Schofield.

"The .44 bullet, would you say it was the cause of death of the victim?" Murphy asked.

"He was hit in the right shoulder by the .50-90 and the bullet did enough damage that it would have killed him eventually," Adams said. "The .44 put the poor bastard out of his misery."

"I need to keep these," Murphy said.

"The bullets? I don't need them," Adams said.

"Thanks, Doctor."

Walking back to the marshal's office, Murphy said, "I'm going to check into the Dodge Hotel, grab a nap, and then have dinner in their restaurant. Are you free to join me?"

"What time?"

"Seven okay?"

"See you then."

"Oh, I almost forgot. Where is the telegraph office?"

"Three storefronts down from my office."

"I need to send a wire to Washington. I'd appreciate it if you came with me."

"Afternoon, Marshal," Olson said from behind the telegraph operator's desk.

"Olson, this is Mr. Murphy," Poule said. "He needs to send a wire."

Olson picked up the telegraph pad and said, "Fill out what you want to say and to who and . . ."

"I need to do it myself," Murphy said.

"Yourself?"

"I'm not authorized to give you the code for the President," Murphy said.

"The president of what?" Olson asked.

"He means Garfield, Olson," Poule said.

Olson looked up at Murphy. "President Garfield?"

"That's the one," Poule said.

"Can you operate a . . . ?" Olson said.

"I can," Murphy said.

Olson stood up, stepped aside, and allowed Murphy to take his seat.

"I still need a record of your transaction," Olson said.

"I can't do that," Murphy said. "And I need you to leave the office."

"Come on, Olson, we'll wait outside," Poule said.

Once Olson and Poule were outside, Murphy began to tap the Morse code key. He began with the secret code to the White House operator and then sent the following message: *From Murphy Stop Dodge RR and Santa Fe RR back to work Stop Am proceeding to closest site of incident with settlers Stop Making some progress Stop Do not reply Stop Murphy*

Murphy stood up and went outside where Olson and Poule were standing on the wood sidewalk.

"Thank you, Mr. Olson," Murphy said.

"Do you want me to bring you a reply?" Olson asked.

"There won't be one."

Murphy checked into a room on the third floor of the Dodge Hotel. He requested a room that faced the back alley so he could open the window and not hear noises from the busy street below.

He locked the door, stripped down to his underwear, lit his pipe, and opened his notebook on the bed.

The .44 Schofield didn't match his .45

Schofield for power, but it had one advantage in that it was a bit more accurate at a longer distance. Both broke open, automatically ejected the spent shells, and made reloading much quicker than a gate-loaded handgun.

About thirty seconds quicker.

If you're on horseback and in a skirmish thirty seconds can seem a lifetime. That was one reason the Army chose the Schofield .44 over the Colt .45 for its soldiers.

Murphy flipped the notebook to a clean page.

The .44 Schofield used by the US Army and also the Russian Army and others.

The Sharps rifle was used by military snipers.

Murphy remembered carrying the Sharps during the war when he trained as a sniper. Later, when it was introduced in 1873, he purchased a .44 Schofield revolver, but later traded it in for the more powerful .45 version. Both were far superior to the Navy 1860 cap and ball revolver he carried during the war, which was slow to load and useless when the powder was wet.

Possibility the shooter is a former Army cavalryman or sniper.

Murphy closed the notebook, set the pipe aside, and took a nap.

■ ■ ■ ■

"How is your steak, Marshal?" the waitress at the Dodge Hotel dining room asked.

"Fine, Janie, just fine," Poule said.

She looked at Murphy.

"And yours?"

"Real good, thank you."

"Let me know if you need anything else."

After Janie left the table, Murphy asked, "How many settlers have been killed in your jurisdiction in Kansas?"

"Seven as far as I know," Poule said. "A family of three near Tyler City about seventy miles from here and a family of four north of Two Ridge. Farmers looking for a new life wound up with no life at all."

"The Army handle that?"

Poule nodded.

"Who commands Fort Dodge?"

"Colonel Henry Flynt."

"I'll be seeing him first thing in the morning if you'd care to tag along."

"If nothing comes up overnight I'll take a ride with you."

Murphy nodded. "How is the dessert here?" he asked.

He saw his wife for the last time the morning

he left to report to the Army. Her face was young and freshly scrubbed from a hot bath. Her long hair was draped around her shoulders and in the dim light in their bedroom it appeared as if she wore a shawl over her naked shoulders.

They made love while the baby slept and afterward she fixed him breakfast and packed a lunch for the long ride into town.

He promised to write every week, but of course he didn't. Once a month on average was the best he could manage while in training. She wrote every week, but the mail was slow to the field and sometimes it would be months before her letters caught up to him, sometimes a dozen at once. When he was promoted and took over a sniper squad he wrote but twice in six months. He told himself and her that he took the promotion for the extra money to send home, and he did faithfully send most of his pay back to her.

But it was a lie.

Murphy opened his eyes, sat up, and gasped loudly for air.

He was drenched in sweat and shivering.

The room was almost completely dark. A sliver of light from the moon could be seen through the window.

Murphy got off the bed and lit the oil lamp on the desk against the wall. He opened his satchel and removed the bottle of his father's whiskey, pulled the cork, and took a long hard drink, needing several more to return to sleep.

EIGHT

Murphy rented a horse at the Dodge Livery and left with Poule at sunrise for Fort Dodge. The ride was four miles to the north and they rode at a leisurely pace and covered the distance in under an hour.

The sixteen-foot-high gates were closed when they arrived at the fort. Four sentinels patrolled the catwalk, one for each direction.

The gates faced to the south and the soldier on lookout called down to Poule and Murphy.

"Marshal Poule, what brings you to Fort Dodge?" the soldier asked.

"To see the colonel," Poule said. "This is Mr. Murphy from Washington. He needs to speak with Colonel Flynt."

The soldier turned and looked down into the interior of the fort. "Open the gates," he ordered.

Murphy and Poule joined Colonel Flynt and his staff of six officers in the officers' mess hall for breakfast.

The much larger mess hall for the two hundred soldiers and noncommissioned officers was located directly across the wide central street of the fort.

"So how are things in Washington these days, Mr. Murphy?" Flynt asked.

"Everybody on the Hill hates everybody else and given half the chance every last one of them would stab Garfield in the back to win reelection," Murphy said.

"So nothing has changed," Flynt said.

"Only some of the names, Colonel."

Flynt, sipping coffee, nodded. He set the cup down and said, "You didn't ride out here to tell me construction of the Santa Fe continued."

"No."

"Although I must admit that is no small feat," Flynt said. "Anyway, what can I do for you that you're so far away from home?"

"It concerns the murdered settlers," Murphy said.

Flynt sighed. "Nasty business."

"Yes."

"Can we discuss this in my office after breakfast?"

"Certainly."

Colonel Flynt's office was located opposite the main barracks. It was large enough to house his desk and a desk for an on-duty secretary when the colonel was in. A large map of the United States and its territories hung behind Flynt's desk. A woodstove, cabinets, and chairs complemented the two desks.

"This is Sergeant Grimes," Flynt said when the sergeant came to attention as Flynt, Murphy, and Poule entered the office. "At ease, Sergeant."

Grimes relaxed. "Coffee, Colonel? I just made it."

"Yes, for all of us," Flynt said. "And then pull all reports on the murdered settlers."

"Yes, Colonel."

"Captain Greenly led a detail of twenty-four men to the north to investigate the family of three," Flynt said. "Lieutenant Ash took a detail southwest to gather details on the family of four."

"Here you go, Colonel," Grimes said and set a tray with three mugs on the table. "I'll get those reports."

Murphy and Poule lifted their mugs.

Grimes returned with two thick files.

"Give them to him," Flynt said and nodded to Murphy.

Grimes handed the files to Murphy.

"Go get breakfast before it's all gone," Flynt said.

"Yes, Colonel," Grimes said and left the office.

Murphy read Greenly's report first. The sheriff of Tyler City reported the dead family of three to Flynt. It was brought to the sheriff's attention by drovers taking cattle to Dodge when they stumbled upon their covered wagon on the plains. The dead bodies were scattered near the wagon. The family of husband, wife, and boy of about ten were black. It is not known if at one time the man and woman were slaves or not. A log book of their journey started in Minneapolis, Minnesota, and ended on the plains of Kansas, hundreds of miles from their final destination, a farm they purchased from the government in Colorado.

A bill of sale and five hundred dollars in paper money was found in a box inside the wagon. Nothing apparently was taken from the wagon or the victims' clothing.

All three victims had been shot at close range. The man was shot three times, the woman and boy just once.

Murphy looked up. "Who determined they were shot at close range?"

"Major Belle, our doctor," Flynt said. "His report is at the end of the file."

The victims and covered wagon were taken to the fort by Greenly's patrol where they were examined by Doctor Belle.

After examining the victims Belle removed five .44 caliber bullets from them, three from the man. The woman was shot once in the chest, as was the boy, but the man was shot in the right shoulder, left upper back, and finally in the heart at point-blank range.

Murphy closed his eyes for a moment.

The first shot spun him around. The second shot brought him to his knees. The killer walked up to him, placed the gun to his chest, and fired the third bullet.

Murphy set the file on the desk and opened the second one written by Lieutenant Ash. He took his command to Two Ridge where the sheriff had taken the bodies of the four victims.

According to the sheriff, the four consisted of husband and wife, son and daughter. Ages of the children were put at around ten and twelve by the local doctor in town. He removed the bullet from the man and woman, but not the children. The caliber

119

was identified by the sheriff as .50-90 Sharps.

The covered wagon they were traveling in wasn't touched. Money, jewelry, clothing, and food supplies were intact when the sheriff and his deputies arrived on the scene.

The family was having a picnic lunch on a blanket when they were shot and killed. The children died last. They were able to run about twenty feet before they were shot in the back.

The family was buried in Boot Hill outside of Two Ridge.

Murphy looked at Flynt. "So the doctor never examined the family of four before they were buried?"

"No."

"Have you investigated any other incidents such as these?"

"The first series of shootings at the railroad in Dodge and Santa Fe."

"Your doctor examine?"

"Yes."

"I'd like to see him now."

Major Belle had been an Army doctor since the first shot fired in the Civil War, almost twenty years ago.

Murphy was surprised to see that Belle wasn't yet fifty years old, much younger than he expected. He had to wait in an exterior waiting room for thirty minutes as Belle was operating on a young soldier with a ruptured appendix.

Finally, a nurse in white entered the waiting room and escorted Murphy to Belle's office at the end of the hospital.

"I'm Doctor Belle," Belle said. "The Colonel tells me you want to talk to me about the railroad shootings."

"Yes."

"Well, have a seat," Belle said and moved to a seat behind his desk.

Murphy took one of three chairs facing the desk.

"What about the railroad shootings?" Belle asked.

"The first group of shootings is the one I'm interested in," Murphy said. "What can you tell me about them?"

"I wasn't there, of course," Belle said. "I can tell you that they were all shot at long range with what the gunnery sergeant identified as .50-90 ammunition. The damage done to these men was something I haven't seen since the war."

"Did you save the bullets after you removed them?"

"Yes."

"Can I see them?"

Belle stood up from his desk and walked across the office to a chest. He opened the large door and removed a glass jar and returned to the desk with it. He set it on the desk and said, "Nine bullets in all, most of them destroyed on impact."

Murphy dumped the bullets on the desk.

"Can I have some pencils, please?" he asked.

Under the microscope in Belle's examination room he studied the .50-90 shell casing and a bullet from the jar.

"That's the man's fingerprints?" Belle said as he peered through the lens.

"Yes."

"One appears to be a thumb and the other his forefinger."

"Do you have some clean white paper?"

"Of course."

After shaving graphite onto the paper, Murphy rolled the shell casing over it and then made another pile to the right of the first. He rolled the slug over the graphite and then placed casing and slug on the desk.

"I need a waste basket or bucket," Murphy said.

Belle removed the wood wastebasket from

under his desk and placed it beside Murphy.

Murphy lifted the paper and gently shook it over the wastebasket until most of the graphite fell off the paper.

Two black stains remained on the paper.

Murphy set the paper on the desk, held it in place, and gently blew on the stains until dust particles blew off and the fingerprints appeared as wavy black lines and grooves.

"I'll be damned," Belle said. "I've never seen that done before."

"Can I have an envelope, the kind used for mailing a letter?"

Belle opened his desk and gave Murphy an envelope. Carefully folding the paper, Murphy inserted the paper into the envelope.

"Thank you, doctor," he said.

Murphy and Poule rode back to Dodge City and arrived close to noon. Poule waited with Murphy at the train depot for Bradley's private train to arrive and take Murphy back to the railroad camp.

"What now?" Poule asked.

"I keep on his trail," Murphy said. "Check out more sites where he's killed. Look for more clues and witnesses. Eventually the circle tightens around him. Nobody, not even him, can hide forever."

"I can check with other marshals and sheriffs by wire for anything new," Poule said. "How long do you plan to be at the camp?"

"A day or so," Murphy said. "Then I'll check on the Santa Fe camp and move on from there."

"If I get any new information I'll ride out and bring it to you."

"Much appreciated."

Looking down the platform, Poule said, "I see the train coming."

What links railroad workers to settlers moving west?

On the surface, nothing.

Below the surface, nothing.

The two groups have nothing in common.

Nothing, except they were all murdered by the same hand.

What was their crime?

What did they do to the killer to deserve their fate?

Murphy closed his notebook and stood as the train slowed to a stop in the Dodge City railroad camp.

"Four miles of new track and the men have

agreed to work through the night," Bradley said.

"What about Santa Fe?" Murphy asked.

"Close to the same," Bradley said. "Both camps agree that the goal is to link the two by mid-summer, and the major investors have agreed to an added bonus for all men if this is accomplished."

They were having dinner in Bradley's private dining car. Parker, after serving, joined them.

"It's amazing how quickly men will work knowing armed guards are protecting them," Bradley said.

"Not so amazing," Murphy said. "During the war the Army engineers could construct a bridge overnight when they had a full squad of men standing guard. Alone and without protection the same engineers would take a week."

"You knew the men would react that way?" Bradley said.

"Yes."

"So where do you go from here?"

"Santa Fe in the morning," Murphy said. "Then follow the bodies until something breaks or I get a new lead."

Parker looked at Murphy. "Mr. Murphy, do you play chess?"

"I do."

"Care for a game after dinner?"

"Why not?"

After forty-seven moves the game was setting itself up for a draw. Neither Murphy nor Parker had a clear advantage in attack, defense, or pieces.

"You play an excellent game, Mr. Parker," Murphy said.

"As do you."

"Where did you learn to play?"

"On the plantation," Parker said. "The owner insisted that all house slaves be as educated as possible."

"Did you play him much?"

"All the time."

"Did you ever beat him?"

"Every game," Parker said and touched his head. "In here."

"Did he ever beat you?"

"Every game."

Parker smiled.

Murphy looked at Parker.

"I may have only been a house slave, but I wasn't stupid."

Murphy nodded and then studied the board.

"The only real way to win is to learn your opponent and if he thinks ten moves ahead you try to think twelve," Parker said.

Murphy looked up from the board. "I propose a draw, Mr. Parker."

"As do I, Mr. Murphy."

Both toppled their kings.

"Mr. Murphy, please come to breakfast."

Alone in his tent, Murphy opened his notebook and turned up the light in the oil lamp and wrote a notation.

Anticipate his moves.

Murphy closed the notebook and lay down on his cot and stared at the ceiling of his tent.

Soft piano music filtered into the tent. He listened for a moment and then stood up, turned down the lamp, and walked outside. The music was louder and he followed it to the large tent that served as the saloon. He walked past the saloon to the end of camp to Bradley's private train. Several oil lamps were lit inside the main car.

Murphy climbed the steps to the platform and knocked on the door.

Wearing a blue silk robe, Bradley answered the door.

"Mr. Murphy, is something wrong?"

"How many other railroad lines are under construction out west?" Murphy asked.

"I'm not sure," Bradley said. "Several at least that I'm aware of, probably more."

"Can you find out exactly?"

"I can send a wire and find out in the morning."

"Thank you. Goodnight."

"Hold on for a second," Bradley said. "What's on your mind, Mr. Murphy?"

"Chess."

NINE

The piano music drew Murphy to the saloon on the way back to his tent from Bradley's train.

Near the saloon was Sally's large tent. It was well lit with oil lamps and he could hear voices and laughter from inside.

Murphy paused, turned, hesitated, and then ducked inside Sally's tent. Six men and six of Sally's girls immediately fell silent at the sight of him.

"I'm looking for Sally," Murphy said.

"She ain't here right now," one of the girls said.

Murphy nodded. "Tell her Murphy stopped by to say goodbye."

"Sure."

Murphy stepped outside and walked past the saloon, turned and headed for his tent. As he went past rows and rows of tents very few were illuminated from within.

As he neared his tent, light from the oil

lamp shone brightly through the canvas.

But he had lowered the flame, hadn't he?

Murphy grabbed the flap, flipped it open, and stepped inside the tent.

Sally was in the chair at the small table. She was drinking a glass of Murphy's father's whiskey. The bottle was on the table next to an extra glass.

"That's a new bottle," Murphy said as he walked to the table.

"I took a ride into Dodge and went to every saloon until I found one," Sally said. "Expensive stuff."

Murphy sat and poured a drink.

"I'm leaving in the morning," he said.

Sally took a sip. "I know."

"I would have said goodbye first."

"I know that, too," Sally said. "I figured I would get it over with now."

Murphy lifted his glass and took a sip.

So did Sally. "Your father knows his craft."

"Forty-five years perfecting it."

"Where are you off to?"

"Santa Fe first, then I'm not sure. Wherever the clues take me."

"You don't make it easy on a woman, do you?"

"I don't make it easy on myself," Murphy said.

"I see that. Why?"

Murphy sipped his father's whiskey. "My wife and child were murdered in sixty-four by deserters who invaded our farm while I was off fighting the war. I didn't get home until almost sixty-six and by then they were in the ground two years. I spent the next three years hunting down the men who did it and I executed every one of them."

Sally stared at Murphy.

"I can understand what you did given what you told me, but I can't understand your guilt over what happened," she said. "A lot of that happened during the war."

Murphy tossed back the rest of his drink and then poured another.

"The war hadn't reached us yet," he said. "And the truth is I went off to fight because I couldn't stand being behind a plow one more day. I didn't so much join the Army as desert my wife. And every day in that war no matter how bloody and gruesome was better than plowing a field. That guilt you spoke of is not because I joined the war, but because I abandoned my family."

With mist in her eyes Sally reached out to touch Murphy on his cheek. Then she stood up and started to walk to the flap of the tent.

"Wait," Murphy said. "Don't go."

Sally turned and looked at Murphy.

"Are you sure?"

"Yes."

Ten

Murphy rode out of the Dodge City camp shortly after sunrise and headed south to the Santa Fe camp on a well-rested Boyle. In the previous two days the Santa Fe camp had moved ten or more miles north, cutting a half day's ride off the trip.

Bradley rode his train into Dodge to send the telegram to his home office for the information on new tracks being built around the west. He hoped to have a detailed answer by the time Murphy reached the Santa Fe camp.

By nightfall Murphy had covered a third of the way. He rewarded Boyle with carrots and sugar cubes as he brushed and groomed him.

After a quick supper of beans, bacon, biscuits, and coffee, Murphy sat by the campfire and opened his notebook.

Chess.

A game of wits, skill, experience, and

knowledge.

Learn your opponent.

Learn how he thinks and anticipate his moves.

Be there when he moves again.

Murphy closed the notebook.

He tossed a few extra sticks onto the campfire and then got into his bedroll.

Be there when he moves again, he thought.

It's the only way you're going to stop him.

Sally crept into his thoughts. They had made love twice that night and once again in the morning. She had awakened something that had been buried deep inside him for a very long time.

Passion.

They shared coffee before he rode out. She told him that as soon as the connector was finished she would return to Saint Louis and that she hoped he would visit her there as soon as his business was concluded.

As he looked up at the stars, fear of his weakness came back to haunt. He feared that given the chance he would rather be in Sally's bed than on the road.

That distraction could get a man killed when a man's profession dealt with life and death.

Murphy rode into the Santa Fe camp after

134

dark. Work had ceased for the day. The mess tent was full, as was the saloon.

Murphy dismounted and walked Boyle to the far end where Johnson's private car was located.

Lights shone through the windows. Murphy tied Boyle to the guard rail, then climbed to the platform and knocked on the door.

Moy opened the door, recognized Murphy, smiled, and stepped aside.

Johnson was having dinner at the conference table where several large maps were spread out in front of him.

"Mr. Murphy, please come in and join me," Johnson said.

Murphy went to the table and glanced at the maps before he took a seat.

Moy set a plate and tea in front of Murphy and filled the plate with beef, vegetables, white rice, and toasted almonds. A plate of chicken dumplings with sauce was on a separate plate.

"We've made good progress in the past few days," Johnson said. "Without any more delays we should link with the Dodge project inside of a month."

Murphy ate a dumpling.

"In addition, I've hired on fifty new men," Johnson said.

"Good to hear. Can you give me a ride into Santa Fe in the morning?" Murphy asked.

"Of course," Johnson said. "And please use the extra bedroom in my car tonight. With the new men I'm short on tents."

Murphy nodded and dug into the beef.

"If I may ask, from Santa Fe to where next?" Johnson asked.

"Not sure," Murphy said as he forked beef and vegetables into his mouth. He chewed and swallowed and sipped tea. "I've asked Mr. Bradley to check on new railroad lines being constructed. Maybe you can find out as well."

Johnson nodded. "New lines mean new potential victims," he said. "Of course."

Murphy nodded at the maps. "These maps are of what?"

"The original plans for the route to Dodge City," Johnson said. "We might have to make some adjustments right around here where our original route was mapped. Tracks were set down, but the work might be redirected."

Johnson circled a spot on the map with his finger.

"Why?" Murphy asked.

"The shortest route from Santa Fe to Dodge cuts through this range," Johnson said. "It belongs to a rancher named Kasem and three years ago he sold the rights to the land to the Santa Fe Railroad. Apparently now he's changed his mind."

"Because?"

"He's seventy-one or two and had retired from ranching," Johnson said. "His sons returned home a year or so ago and have reactivated the ranch and they need the land for grazing. If we can't settle this dispute quickly, we may have to move twenty miles to the northeast to complete the route."

"Does Bradley know about this?"

"I wired him yesterday."

"What are you going to do about it?"

"Go see Mr. Kasem, see if we can reach an agreement."

"When?"

"I was planning on first light tomorrow," Johnson said. "It's a ten-mile ride to the end of the track and just a few hundred yards to the Kasem property line. I'd like to be there by noon."

"I'll go with you."

"That won't be necessary. I'll have Mr. Swan and a dozen armed men with me."

"That may be true, but your employer is private," Murphy said. "Mine is the US government and I may be of some use in negotiations. A day's delay to Santa Fe won't hurt my plans none at all. We'll leave before dawn and have breakfast on the train," Murphy said. "The boxcar can hold fifteen horses, so one more won't hurt."

Murphy turned and looked at Moy, who had taken a seat to his left. "Mr. Moy, do you know how to make pancakes? I have a feel for pancakes for breakfast."

"I can make anything you wish," Moy said.

"Good," Murphy said. He looked at Johnson. "Show me that map again."

After enjoying a leisurely ride and a fine breakfast of pancakes with bacon and toast, Murphy, Johnson, Swan, and a dozen armed railroad men saddled their horses, put them in the boxcar, and rode Johnson's train ten miles to the site on the map.

The ride took just over ninety minutes.

At the site where the tracks were marked to be continued, a hundred head of cattle grazed on tall grass.

To the left of the field, about five hundred yards away stood the Kasem ranch house. Murphy, Johnson, Swan, and the railroad men retrieved their horses in preparation for the ride to the Kasem ranch house.

"See those hills on our right?" Johnson asked. "We would have to go around them and that would add twenty miles to the route, not to mention the added time of three weeks, extra payroll in the thousands, and expenses in track and supplies."

"I see what you mean," Murphy said.

"Riders coming, Mr. Johnson," Swan said.

Three men were riding from the ranch house to the field.

Johnson removed binoculars from his saddlebags and looked at the riders.

"The one in the middle is Mr. Kasem," he said. "The other two must be his sons."

"Should we meet them?" Swan asked.

"No."

While they waited for Kasem and his sons to arrive, Murphy filled his pipe and lit it with a wood match.

When they arrived at the field, Kasem said, "You're trespassing on my land."

"I'm . . ." Johnson said.

"I remember who you are," Kasem said.

"Then you remember the railroad leased this land from you in seventy-eight," Johnson said.

"Before my sons came home," Kasem said. "And after almost three years of you doing nothing, I figure our deal is concluded."

"You figured wrong," Johnson said.

The son to Kasem's right said, "I'd be happy to shoot this son of a bitch, Pa."

"I don't advise that," Murphy said.

"Who are you?" Kasem said.

"Name is Murphy. I'm with the government sent from Washington to . . ."

The hole exploded in Kasem's chest three to four seconds before the rifle shot sounded. He was on the ground before the echo faded and by then the son to the right was blown off his horse.

"Dismount! Take cover!" Murphy shouted.

"Pa! Michael!" the remaining brother yelled just as a bullet nearly took off the top of his head.

The report of the round took four seconds.

As Murphy hit the ground he grabbed his Henry rifle from the saddle sleeve and cocked the lever.

"Jesus Christ, it's him, isn't it?" Johnson said.

"Nobody move," Murphy said. "He's in those hills and can pick us off one at a time if he sees movement."

"Those hills are fifteen hundred yards away," Swan said.

"I counted four seconds for the sound to reach us," Murphy said. "He's there."

"What are we supposed to do, squat in the dirt while he kills us one at a time?" Swan demanded.

"Just don't move and keep your head in the grass," Murphy said. "He can't shoot what he can't see."

Murphy looked at the train about a hundred and fifty feet away. If they made a run for it in the time it took to reach the car, he could easily pick off three, maybe four of them running.

"Mr. Johnson, how much liquor is aboard the train?" Murphy asked.

"A full bar. Why?"

"What's your engineer's name?"

"Jackson."

"Mr. Jackson, can you hear me?" Murphy yelled.

"I hear you."

"Go to the bar and grab four or five full bottles of whiskey and stuff them with linen napkins," Murphy said.

"I don't have the key."

"Moy has it," Johnson yelled.

"All right," Jackson shouted.

While they waited, Johnson peered through his binoculars. "I don't see anything."

"You won't," Murphy said.

"Maybe he left?" Swan said.

"Stand up and find out," Murphy said.

"No thanks," Swan said.

"Okay, Mr. Johnson, I have five bottles of

whiskey and napkins," Jackson shouted. "What now?"

"Light them one at a time and throw them as far into the field as possible," Murphy said.

Murphy flipped up the sights on the Henry rifle and when the first bottle flew out of the train, he waited until the bottle was descending and then fired a shot. The bottle exploded and sent flames scattering across the grass.

By the time the fifth bottle was thrown, the field was engulfed in high, quickly spreading flames.

The cattle, spooked by the encroaching fire, started to scatter quickly.

"The smoke and heat rising from the fire will give us cover," Murphy said. "Grab any horse and run to the boxcar. Now!"

Led by Murphy, each man jumped up and raced to the horses, grabbed one, and ran them to the boxcar. Once the horses were safely in the car, they climbed aboard Johnson's private car.

"Everybody stay here," Murphy said. "And don't look out the window."

Murphy opened the door and crossed the platform to the engine car where Jackson sat behind the controls.

"Take us out of here slow," Murphy said.

"Go about one mile and stop."

"The whole field's burning," Jackson said.

"I wasn't asking, Mr. Jackson."

"Right. One mile."

Murphy returned to the private car.

"Mr. Johnson, once I'm off the train tell Mr. Jackson full throttle back to camp," Murphy said. "I'll see you later tonight."

"You're not going after that lunatic?" Johnson asked.

"I need a little exercise after breakfast."

Murphy opened the door and entered the boxcar. The horses were skittish and he rubbed Boyle's neck to calm him.

"It's all right, big fellow," Murphy said. "I'd never do you any harm, you know that. I just need you to do something for me is all."

The train rolled slowly backward along the track. Murphy replaced the Henry rifle in the sleeve.

After ten minutes or so the train stopped. Murphy slid the door of the boxcar open and then mounted Boyle.

"Let's do it," Murphy said and jumped Boyle out of the car to the ground.

Murphy held Boyle fast for a moment as he scanned the hills a mile away.

"Now show me something," Murphy said and kicked Boyle into high gear.

Racing toward the hills at forty miles per hour, Murphy didn't slow Boyle until they reached the foothills and then he took Boyle down to a slow trot and finally a walk.

Murphy dismounted and rubbed Boyle's neck.

"Well, he didn't shoot at us," Murphy said. "Catch your breath and we'll go up for a look around."

Once Boyle's breathing returned to normal, Murphy held him by the reins and they slowly climbed the hill to the top.

On the flat plateau Murphy selected a poplar tree beside some sweet grass and removed his rope from the saddle clip. He formed a loop and placed it around Boyle's neck and tied the other end around the poplar. Boyle had about fifteen feet of room to move about and eat grass.

"I won't be long," Murphy said, and patted Boyle's neck.

Murphy drew his .45 and held it loosely by his side as he started walking the plateau. He walked for about five hundred yards before he found what he was looking for.

Fastened out of sticks and leather strips, the shooter had made a tripod to rest the Sharps rifle on for a more accurate shot at so long a distance.

He stood before the tripod and looked

down on the burning fields. The fire would burn all the way to the ranch and hills, consuming everything burnable before it ran out of fuel and extinguished.

He turned and walked to the ashes of a campfire. The ashes were still warm. Beside the ashes was a deep impression in the grass made by a bedroll.

Not far away, Murphy checked manure piles and estimated the shooter had camped out for four days.

He was waiting for the railroad to reach this point.

Stalking and waiting for new victims.

Murphy holstered the .45 and started walking back to Boyle.

Murphy reached the Santa Fe railroad camp by late afternoon. As he dismounted and walked Boyle into camp a crowd of men followed him to Johnson's private car.

By the time he reached the car, nearly every man in the camp had surrounded him.

Johnson appeared on the platform of his car.

"Mr. Murphy, I've informed the men of the shooting this morning," Johnson said. "Would you care to hear the response?"

"I would."

"Mr. Munro, would you tell Mr. Murphy

the decision of the men."

Munro pushed through the crowd and stood in front of Murphy.

"After what you did today, all of us would be cowards if we stopped work," Munro said. "We decided and Mr. Johnson agrees that we can work just as hard and cover just as much ground working at night with lanterns. At least the shooter won't have a clear shot at night, don't you agree?"

"I do," Murphy said.

"Mr. Murphy, come have dinner with me," Johnson said.

Munro took the reins from Murphy. "I'll see he's taken proper care of," Munro said.

"I sent a wire to Mr. Bradley in the Dodge camp and he's agreed to work at night," Johnson said. "I also informed the marshal of the murder of the Kasem family. If this son of a bitch comes back, he won't find a clean shot so easy."

"A full moon gives a nice target of moving shadow on shadow," Murphy said. "Place extra torches fifteen feet from the tracks and the light will block his night vision. Do it on both sides."

"You know about such things," Johnson said.

"I've had some experience in the matter."

146

Moy wheeled a large serving cart from the kitchen.

"Chicken and beef dumplings, rice with almonds, seasoned steak, snap peas, and tea," Moy said.

After Moy served, he filled a third plate and sat beside Johnson.

"Have you gotten any information on other railroads under construction?" Murphy asked.

"Between Mr. Bradley and I, we've compiled quite a list."

"Good."

Murphy ate a beef dumpling.

"Mr. Moy, after dinner, how about coffee and dessert?"

■ ■ ■ ■

The sleeping car was as fine as any hotel room on Capitol Hill. The bed was large enough for two and exceptionally comfortable. Crystal lanterns adorned the walls as did several paintings.

Murphy stripped down and got under the covers. He extinguished the lamp on the bedside table and moonlight filtered in through the open window.

He was exhausted and sleep should have been almost immediate, but as he started to drift off thoughts of Sally entered his mind.

The softness of her body, the scent of her hair, the way she pressed herself against him, he saw her in his mind and could almost feel her touch.

He rolled over and looked at the pale moonlight shining through the window. It cast shadows against the wall.

Put her out of your mind.

She's a distraction and a man in his position couldn't afford any distractions, no matter how slight or pleasant.

A distraction gave the shooter the advantage.

Murphy looked up at the ceiling.

He closed his eyes and forced sleep to shut him down.

ELEVEN

After checking into the Hotel Santa Fe, Murphy took a table in the dining hall and ordered a large lunch.

He read reports from Bradley and Johnson as he ate.

The expansion of the modern era had taken root in the country and eleven other railroad routes were under construction. Some as short as forty miles to link major cities, others as far as a thousand miles or more to link northern states with southern.

With the expansion of the railroad the country shrunk. An east coast to west journey that used to take three months or more now took just six days on the Iron Horse.

The shooter could pick any new railroad route to stake out fresh targets. The same could be said for new settlements. Underpopulated territories needed larger populations to achieve statehood. They needed farmers, ranchers, and industrial pioneers. With the shooter murdering entire families, the movement west had slowed to almost a standstill.

The question was, where would he strike next?

While Murphy was contemplating the question, the hotel desk clerk entered the dining hall with a message.

"Mr. Murphy, telegram from the US Marshal in Dodge City," he said and handed Murphy the sealed envelope.

After the clerk left, Murphy tore open the envelope and read the telegram.

Family of five murdered in Guymon, Oklahoma Stop Contact me at once for details Stop Marshal Poule

Murphy folded the telegram into a pocket, and then finished his lunch.

When Murphy entered the Santa Fe Railroad office located at the end of the depot, telegraph operator Baker looked at him and said, "You again."

"Mr. Baker," Murphy said.

"Do you want to send a telegram or see Mr. Potts?" Baker asked.

"Both. First, is Mr. Potts around?"

"He went to Chicago on railroad business," Baker said. "What about the telegram?"

"Send it, although it might take awhile for a response."

Baker nodded.

"Address US Marshal Poule, Dodge City. Stop. Await information. Stop. Murphy."

"That's it?"

"I'll wait around for the response if you want to lunch," Murphy said.

Murphy drank two cups of coffee from the pot Baker had warming on the woodstove and smoked two bowls on his pipe before Dodge City replied.

From US Marshal Poule Stop Family of five shot at long range with 50-90 Sharps Stop Family purchased farm outside Guymon, Oak Stop Poule.

Murphy immediately replied.

From Murphy Stop How long before bodies found and by whom Stop

A few minutes passed before the reply came.

From US Marshal Poule Stop Bodies found by clerk delivering chicken wire to farm Stop Doctor in Guymon estimated dead five days Stop

Murphy replied.

From Murphy Stop Thank you Stop.

■ ■ ■ ■

Murphy spread his map out on the desk in his hotel room. As he smoked his pipe he studied New Mexico, Oklahoma, and Kansas. The western part of Oklahoma sliced directly into the path of the Santa Fe to Dodge route. The town of Guymon was between the two points. He found new victims in the family of five and then rode south and three days later murdered the Kasem family north of Santa Fe.

Murphy looked up from the map.

He opened his notebook.

The son of a bitch made a loop.

He closed the notebook and left the room.

At the depot ticket window, Murphy stepped up to the clerk and said, "The next train to Washington DC leaves when?"

"Tomorrow morning at ten if it's on time."

"Let me have a one-way ticket."

After purchasing the ticket, Murphy returned to Baker's office where the clerk was receiving a telegram.

After he was done copying the message, Baker looked at Murphy.

"This one you'll have to wait outside," Murphy said.

"Classified?"

"Afraid so."

Baker stood and walked outside.

Murphy sat and sent a message.

From Murphy Stop To White House Special Assistant William Burke Stop Will see you in three days Stop

TWELVE

"I must admit that I had my doubts about you, but from all accounts the Santa Fe to Dodge project will be completed nearly on time thanks to you," Burke said.

"He's not going to stop," Murphy said. "He's killing with a vengeance and he won't stop until he's satisfied or he's dead."

They were in the den of Murphy's home in Virginia. Each man sipped Murphy's father's whiskey.

Murphy smoked his pipe.

"The country is too big for me to hunt him down without knowing who I'm after," Murphy said. "Like a needle in a haystack."

"Why do I have the feeling you want something," Burke said.

"One hundred percent access to all military records," Murphy said.

"Why?" Burke asked. "He isn't targeting the Army."

"I witnessed him kill three men from

fifteen hundred yards," Burke said. "There's only one place a man learns a skill like that."

Burke nodded. "All right. Anything else?"

"I'll let you know."

"I'll speak with the President and the War Department in the morning."

"Tell them I'm not asking."

Burke couldn't stop a grin.

"Another drink before you leave?"

"Why not?"

Colonel Nelson rode to Murphy's home the following morning. He was under orders from Garfield to cooperate with Murphy and give him anything he required no matter how classified the material.

Nelson wanted to retire a General and in peace time he knew the only way that would happen would be to capture the eye of the President. He was fifty-three years old and if war did somehow break out in the near future he knew he was too old and tired for a field command. He was to spend the rest of his career polishing a chair and he knew it, but maybe he could ride this chair to a General's star.

Murphy answered the door himself and stood a good six inches taller than Nelson.

"Breakfast, Colonel?" Murphy asked. "I made enough for two."

"That would be good," Nelson said.

For so imposing a figure, Murphy spoke softly as he served breakfast in his kitchen. Scrambled eggs, bacon and sausage, fried potatoes, toast with jam, orange juice and coffee, and all perfectly prepared and served.

"The President has assigned me to you and I am at your disposal," Nelson said. "So, tell me why I am here besides to eat your breakfast."

"I am after a killer, a murderer of men, women, and children," Murphy said.

"I thought you were a congressman," Nelson said.

"Part-time."

Nelson stared across the table at the very rough, very imposing figure of Murphy.

"All right, how can I help you?"

"I believe the man I'm after is a former Army sniper," Murphy said.

"This is about the railroad and settlers, isn't it?"

"Yes."

"And you think an Army sniper is responsible?"

"Former Army sniper."

"Good God, man, do you know what you're saying?"

"He's using a .50-90 Sharps rifle and killing at very long distances," Murphy said. "I witnessed him kill three men at 1500 yards. I was a sniper in the war and we used the Sharps .50-90 with a 30-inch barrel. I could make a head shot at 1200 yards. With a 34- or 35-inch barrel, 1500 yards is possible in the hands of the right man. You're going to help me find that man."

"How?"

"Collect the files on every man trained as a sniper from 1861 to this year," Murphy said. "I don't believe the killer is on active duty so we can immediately weed them out. He's a large man of my size or larger, so we can eliminate all small men as well. He's left-handed so that narrows the field a bit more. And he's harboring a deeply rooted grudge so maybe he was dishonorably discharged or even imprisoned in Leavenworth or another military prison."

"You want a lot for a free breakfast," Nelson said.

"Colonel, I am almost certain that if I mention to the President what a fine General you would make, it would guarantee you a star before you retire," Murphy said.

Nelson sighed.

"How long will it take you to gather the

records and transport them here?" Murphy asked.

"If I assign six clerks to the task working double shifts, it's possible I could have them to you in a week."

"Assign twelve."

Nelson stared at Murphy.

"I wasn't asking," Murphy said.

Nelson nodded.

"Excellent," Murphy said. "I made some nice apple popovers from my mother's recipe for an after-breakfast treat. Would you care for one with some fresh coffee?"

"Oh, well, why not?" Nelson said.

"The President thought it best I keep you advised of all new developments," Burke said.

Murphy struck a match and lit his pipe.

Burke took a sip of Murphy's father's whiskey and then said, "Two new killings to report. A family of settlers in northern Colorado and a family in eastern Utah. Eleven dead in all. No witnesses. Each family had purchased farmland from the government."

"I told you he wasn't going to stop," Murphy said. "Whatever is fueling his hate is all-consuming to him."

"What about your request?"

"Colonel Nelson sent me a telegram that he will bring a shipment of records tomorrow morning."

"Good. Do you need anything, a few men to help with the research?"

"Nelson and I should be able to handle it."

Burke nodded. "I'll tell the President."

Murphy puffed on his pipe and looked at Burke.

"I wonder if I may have a glass of your father's whiskey before I leave?" Burke asked.

"I can give you a bottle if you'd like," Murphy said.

Burke shrugged. "Why not?"

THIRTEEN

Nelson arrived in time for breakfast with two crates of records marked A to G, and H to Z.

Murphy served breakfast before they opened the first crate. Over coffee they started with A, B, and C.

By noon they had eliminated all men less than six feet tall that were right-handed. Of the files of left-handed men over six feet tall all were honorably discharged and had clean military records.

After lunch they tackled files D through G with the same results.

"You can spend the night in my spare bedroom and we can get an early start in the morning," Murphy said.

"All right," Nelson said.

"Let's break for dinner and we can work a few more hours afterward."

When they quit for the night at ten in the evening, they had worked their way to L and the pile of potential candidates had grown to about forty men.

"I could use a drink before bed to help me sleep," Nelson said.

Murphy grabbed the bottle of his father's whiskey and two glasses and opened the doors to the backyard where a table with four chairs rested on the lawn.

They sat and Murphy filled each glass with whiskey.

Murphy stuffed and lit his pipe.

Nelson took a long swallow of whiskey and sighed with satisfaction.

"I will confess to you but deny publicly if you repeat this, but I spent most of the war half drunk," Nelson said. "Sometimes all drunk."

"From what I observed of the men on both sides of the war there was a lot of that going around," Murphy said. "Grant himself was no teetotaler."

"He had a weakness for champagne," Nelson said. "Did you know that?"

"I guarded him for most of his first and entire second term."

"So you knew of his fierce appetite for the bubbly?"

"I did."

"Unlike Grant, who was as fearless a warrior ever to set foot upon a battlefield, I am a genuine pencil-pusher," Nelson said.

"You made Colonel."

"I am also an ass-kisser."

"I wouldn't say that, Colonel."

"I would."

"Colonel, just stepping onto a battlefield takes courage," Murphy said. "Killing is easy to do. It's the living that can be difficult."

Nelson tossed back the rest of his drink and set the glass on the table. "I believe I will turn in now. Goodnight, Mr. Murphy."

"Goodnight, Colonel."

After lunch the following day, they had completed the files all the way to P.

"I need to ride back to Washington to take care of some paperwork I left undone, but I can return in the morning," Nelson said.

After Nelson left, Murphy took the pile of potential suspects out to the backyard along with a bottle of his father's whiskey and a glass.

He lit his pipe and counted the files.

Fifty-one left-handed men trained as snipers between 1861 and 1879 and were no longer in the Army.

All six feet tall or taller.

Forty-three of them were honorably discharged.

Of the forty-three, twenty-seven served from 1861 to 1867.

Of the eight that were not honorably discharged, four were found guilty of cowardice during the war and hung.

Two of the remaining four were serving ten-year sentences at Leavenworth for theft.

That left two unaccounted for. Murphy hoped this list stayed at two, as rooting them out would be quite the chore.

The next batch of names wouldn't be as lengthy, as the closer you got to the end of the alphabet the less common were the names.

Murphy emptied the glass and filled it again. His pipe had gone out and he dumped the ashes, filled it with fresh tobacco, and struck a match.

He sipped the whiskey as he rifled through the pile of forty-three names.

Nothing jumped out at him.

He started to cross reference the names with where they were from to see if any were from the territories of the shootings.

Six were.

That made them guilty of nothing.

Of the men from 1861 through 1867 he recognized seven names. Men he served with, led into battle, or knew from other sniper squads.

That also meant nothing.

The only thing that meant something was a connection between sniper and bloodthirsty madman.

Something linked the two.

It wasn't visible yet.

But it was there.

Murphy held his glass up high, said, "Dad, you make a hell of a whiskey," and tossed back the drink.

Murphy couldn't stop thinking about Sally Orr. He knew that he had to shut his mind down in order to fall asleep, but he took comfort in thinking about her. It was a very long time since a woman waited for him and the thought of that made him feel if not young, then at least spry.

The smell of her hair, the warmth of her touch, the sight of her full-figured body, it had stayed in his mind and caused an ache in his stomach.

He could seek a release on the Hill where a dozen whorehouses were in service for senators and congressmen, places that most of them took refuge in from time to time.

But he knew that would leave him unsatisfied and wanting Sally even more.

He rolled out of bed, struck a match, and lit the oil lamp on the bedside table. Next to the lamp was a half-full bottle of his father's whiskey.

Murphy grabbed the bottle, pulled the cork, and took a long, burning swallow.

Then he shook her off and cleared his mind and a few minutes later when he extinguished the lamp he was able to keep all thoughts of her in the background and fall asleep.

"I need to use your water closet," Nelson said.

Murphy nodded. "We'll break for lunch when you get back."

Nelson left the den to use the water closet located on the first floor of the house opposite the kitchen.

Murphy was riffling through the pile for the letter Q. They had added eight more names to the list of forty-three men honorably discharged, and honorably discharged or not, the whereabouts and activities of each of them would have to be accounted for. To automatically cross any of them off the list would be negligent on Murphy's part. The pile for Q was small. Names beginning with Q weren't common. There were only a few.

He opened the file for Lieutenant John Quad.

From Ohio. Enlisted in late 1863. Detailed to sniper school in early '64. Discharged in early 1867. From 1865 to his discharge, Quad was assigned to Army posts out west to assist with the Indian pacification necessary to allow settlers to develop the land for farming and ranching.

After he returned home in the spring of 1867, Quad moved his wife, Elizabeth, and his baby daughter, Laura-Ann, to southern New Mexico, to 300 acres of farmland he purchased from the government.

Fifteen months later, just as his first crop of melons was coming to harvest, the Army detail assigned to relocation of landowners arrived at Quad's farm. With the Army detail were representatives of the government who told Quad that the railroad expansion to connect the east coast to the west was underway and they required his land for the project.

Quad was offered the price he paid for the land, plus the estimated value of his first year's crop.

Quad refused.

The government officials told Quad that they would confiscate the land under the laws of eminent domain and gave him one week to vacate the land.

Again, Quad refused.

The Army detail and government men returned in one week. Quad put his considerable sniper skills to use and a day-long battle took place that left seven soldiers dead.

From his place in the hills more than a thousand yards away, the soldiers were help-less to return fire as they had far less power-ful weapons than the Sharps rifle Quad used.

Only when they set fire to the farmhouse did Quad come down and surrender. His wife and daughter were hiding in the concealed root cellar dug under the kitchen and protected by a false floor.

Quad was too late to save them. They died of smoke inhalation.

Quad was arrested by Captain Winters, but not before Quad engaged in a physical confrontation that took six men to subdue him.

Tried and convicted for murder, Quad was sentenced to twelve years hard labor at Leavenworth Prison.

As he read the report written by Captain Winters, Murphy locked in on the page and blocked everything else out. His vision focused on the words as his hearing seemed to diminish.

He didn't notice Nelson had returned

until he called Murphy by name.

Murphy looked up.

"Are you all right?" Nelson asked.

"This is our man," Murphy said and held the file out to Nelson.

"It's Colonel Winters now and he retired in seventy-eight," Nelson said.

"To where?"

"South Carolina I believe."

"Find out."

They were eating sandwiches of cold cuts and sipping beer to wash them down.

"I agree that this Quad is a potential suspect, but why are you so sure it's him?" Nelson asked.

"He's a trained sniper. He has a legitimate beef against the railroad and the settlement program. He lost his family in a fire and was sent to prison in sixty-nine for a dozen years," Murphy said. "The shootings began shortly after he was released. He's had a dozen years to plan his revenge on top of the fact that he's filled with rage and hate and is probably half insane by now. It's him. This is our man."

"You want to talk to Winters about what happened in sixty-eight?"

"How well do you know him?"

"Before he retired Winters spent four

years in Washington as an advisor on Indian relations," Nelson said. "We met at meetings, parties, and such. We know each other."

"That's good enough," Murphy said. "Find where he lives and we'll pay him a visit."

"We'll?"

"He's more apt to open the door to someone he knows."

"All right," Nelson said. "I'll head back to Washington and find out where he lives."

Murphy was grooming Boyle after taking him for an afternoon ride when Nelson entered the barn.

"South Carolina on a farm outside of Orangeburg," Nelson said. "The train can put us to within an afternoon's ride."

Brushing Boyle, Murphy looked at Nelson and said, "We'll leave in the morning."

FOURTEEN

Murphy rented a buggy in Orangeburg and set out with Nelson to the Winters's farm located seventeen miles west of the town.

They rode along a winding dirt road that forked several times and they covered the distance in just over three hours, as it was necessary to rest the two horses several times along the way.

The dirt road forked to another private dirt road that led to the Winters's farm. There was an archway with the name Winters painted in gold lettering. A tenth of a mile from the archway stood the three-story high, white and yellow farmhouse.

Winters lived alone. Close to sixty-years-old, the retired Colonel wore a gray beard and his graying hair to his shoulders. When the buggy arrived at the house, Winters stepped out onto the porch and said, "I can't believe it, Nellie. After all these years."

Stepping out of the buggy, Nelson said,

"So you received my telegram then?"

"Yes, this morning," Winters said. "Come sit on the porch. I made a fresh pot of coffee."

While Winters ducked into the house, Nelson and Murphy took the steps onto the porch where a table with four chairs sat beside a swinging chair.

After Winters returned with a tray that held pot, creamer, sugar, and three cups, he poured and sat.

"I was sorry to hear of your wife's passing," Nelson said.

"That's the reason I retired," Winters said. "To take care of her. The pain is gone, but the memory is still intact."

Nelson nodded. "This is Congressman Murphy. This visit concerns what happened in sixty-eight at the Quad farm in New Mexico during the railroad expansion. Anything you can tell us about him is vital."

"I wrote a detailed report on that," Winters said.

"I read it," Murphy said.

"Then you know what happened."

"I do," Murphy said. "I need to fill in between the lines."

"After thirteen years, why?"

"That's classified information. If I tell you I have to insist upon your secrecy."

"You have it as an officer."

"Have you read any news accounts of these killings on the railroad and along settlements out west?" Murphy said.

"A few. Why? Do you think it's Quad?"

"He was released earlier this year and shortly thereafter the killings started," Murphy said. "He has a grudge against the railroad and the settlements. He is a trained sniper and all the killings have been from a distance of a thousand yards or more and he's left-handed and the killer is left-handed."

"How do you know that?" Winters said.

"One shooting victim survived the initial gunshot. He cut his throat and the cut was made right to left indicating he's left-handed."

Winters nodded. "What do you want to know?"

"You led the detail to Quad's home to tell him the railroad needed his property to run the line through," Murphy said. "How did he react to the news?"

"How would you react?" Winters said. "He fought in the war and then spent almost two years out west during the Indian pacification. After his discharge he moved his family west to the three hundred acres he purchased and broke his back planting a crop and then we show up to throw him out. He was angry and stubborn about leaving. He was given a week by the railroad officials to vacate. He refused. When we returned in a week he was in the hills and started picking us off one at a time. We set fire to the house after we checked for his family, not knowing his wife and daughter were hiding in a root cellar. We just wanted him to surrender without any more killing."

"I read in your report it took six men to subdue him once he came down from the hills," Murphy said.

"At least six men," Winters said. "He was as tall as Abe Lincoln and fifty pounds heavier."

"And he was tried, convicted, and sentenced to twelve years hard labor."

"Considering he killed seven men I think the sentence was fair."

"Did anyone ever answer for the deaths of his wife and daughter?" Murphy asked.

"That was an accident and more his fault for hiding them in the cellar."

"Was setting fire to the house an accident?"

"We had orders to confiscate the property and destroy the house," Winters said. "Do you think we would have set fire to the house knowing his wife and daughter were trapped inside?"

"He shot first?"

"Two of my men dismounted and walked to the house," Winters said. "He shot them from a distance of a thousand yards or more. We never returned fire because we were out of range and I think he knew that. All told he killed seven and wounded three others."

Murphy nodded. "Thank you, Colonel. I don't have any more questions."

■ ■ ■ ■

Waiting for the train to take them north to Washington, Murphy and Nelson ate a light supper in the café across the street from the depot.

"He's our man no doubt," Murphy said.

"Okay, he's our man," Nelson said. "Now what?"

"Find him. Smoke him out. Stop him."

"How?"

"I'm working on that."

Nelson looked out the café window. "Our train's coming," he said.

FIFTEEN

Murphy rode the railroad east from Washington to Provo, Utah, the site of the most recent killings of settlers. He wired the US Marshal in Provo and asked him to meet him at the station when his train arrived.

Murphy was leading Boyle out of the boxcar when a US marshal approached him and said, "I'm Marshal James Ward. Are you Murphy?"

"I am, sir," Murphy said.

Ward was a tall, lean man of about thirty-five or so. He wore black pants, white shirt, and a black vest. A walrus mustache dominated his face. The marshal's badge was pinned to the vest.

"My office is at the end of Main Street," Ward said. "Why don't we talk there?"

Holding Boyle by the reins, Murphy walked with Ward the half mile to Ward's office.

"This is my deputy, Harv Bennet, and County Sheriff Tyler," Ward said when they entered his office. He nodded to Bennet and Tyler. "Mr. Murphy from Washington."

"The marshal told me you're here about the Mormon killings," Tyler said.

"Mormons?" Murphy asked. "What Mormons?"

"The family of seven traveling by covered wagon north to the Mormon camp from Arizona," Tyler said.

"They're pretty upset as you can imagine," Ward said.

"How many are there?" Murphy asked.

"Three hundred, maybe more," Ward said.

"And every one of them more hostile than the other," Tyler said.

"Have you had trouble with them?"

"Not like the old days," Tyler said. "But they're capable of it if provoked."

"I'll be riding out to talk with them," Murphy said. "How far and where is their camp?"

"Twenty miles to the northwest," Tyler said. "The marshal and I will go with you."

"Leave at first light," Murphy said. "Right now I need a bed and a steak."

"The Provo Hotel," Ward said. "I'll walk

you over and fill you in on the shootings over a steak myself."

"How is the steak?" the waitress at the Provo Hotel dining room asked.

"Just fine," Ward said.

"Real good. Can we get our coffee touched up?" Murphy asked.

"Sure can. Got fresh apple pie tonight."

"Sounds good," Ward said.

After the waitress filled the coffee cups and left the table, Murphy said, "So, what's the situation with the Mormons?"

"Family of seven traveling from a Mormon camp in Arizona to the camp in Provo were shot while eating lunch ten miles south of here," Ward said. "They were eating at a portable table in a field about a hundred feet off the road. He picked them off one at a time. Four of them running back to the wagon."

"Who found them?"

"Two men from the Provo Freight Company were hauling supplies to Provo on the road and found them about twenty-four hours later," Ward said. "They brought the bodies to town where Doctor Richards cleansed the wounds and made them presentable before they were claimed by the Mormons. They buried them in their camp.

I guess the father of the slain group was to be their new bishop or something. I'm not sure. I don't understand Mormons all that well."

"Did the doctor recover any of the bullets?"

Ward nodded. "Buffalo gun, no doubt."

"What have the Mormons done?" Murphy said. "They can be hostile when provoked."

"As far as I know they've done nothing," Ward said. "Probably because there is nothing to do."

"Do you have a gunsmith in town?"

"Has a large shop at the end of the block where my office is."

"Will he still be open?"

"Doesn't matter. He lives above the shop."

Ben Stark had moved to Provo as a young man twenty years before and opened his shop in a much smaller location than presently occupied next to the livery stables. Over the years, as his business grew, he changed locations three times before buying the storefront at the end of Main Street.

He was working on repairs when Marshal Ward and Murphy knocked on the locked door and asked to come in.

"Ben, this here is Mr. Murphy from

Washington," Ward said. "He has some questions."

"Questions?" Stark asked.

"What do you know about the Mormon shooting?" Murphy asked.

"Hell, it's all anybody is talking about."

"Do you stock Sharps rifles?"

"I do, but not a lot," Stark said. "Not a lot of Buffalo hunters in these parts. Most use a standard Winchester for mule deer and turkey. Why?"

"He killed the Mormons with a Sharps .50-90, that's why."

"A .50-90? I haven't seen one of those since . . . well, at least five years or so."

"So you don't carry .50-90 ammunition?"

"No need. What Sharps I do have are all .45-70 regular Army issue."

"What about a substitute? If I had spent cartridges and wanted to reload them, what could I use in place of a .50-90?" Murphy asked.

"I suppose you could use any .50 caliber bullet in its place so long as it wasn't larger than .90," Stark said.

Murphy nodded. "Have any customers asked for .50 caliber loads recently?"

"I haven't sold a Sharps rifle in over a year," Stark said. "Same for ammunition."

"Thanks for your time."

"The shooter is a large man," Murphy said. "As tall or taller than me."

"How do you know that?" Ward said. "No one has seen him."

"Evidence," Murphy said. "Any large or tall strangers in town recently?"

"Not that I can think of offhand."

They were in Ward's office. Ward was at his desk, Murphy in a chair.

Murphy stood. "I guess I'll see you in the morning."

"I'll ask the sheriff and my deputy if they noticed any strangers of that size in town," Ward said. "Who knows, maybe they have."

■ ■ ■ ■

Murphy sat by the open window of his room at the Provo Hotel and turned up the flame on the oil lamp on the desk.

He opened his notebook.

He wrote one word.

Ammunition.

Sixteen

The Mormon camp sat on twelve acres of land and was surrounded by a fence made of wood that stood sixteen feet high. Catwalks were patrolled by armed guards. One gate was opened to allow farmers to leave in the morning to work the thousand acres of fields behind the fortress, as well as hunters in search of deer and turkey. The gate was then closed and locked shut until farmers and hunters returned.

Murphy, Ward, and Tyler rode to the gate and looked up at the guards on the catwalk.

"What's your business here?" a guard asked with almost a snarl.

"I'm Marshal Ward from Provo. This is Sheriff Tyler and Mr. Murphy from Washington," Ward said. "We'd like to speak to whoever is in charge about the recent killings of that Mormon family on the road."

"Stay on your horses," the guard said.

"Any man dismounts will be shot."

The gates opened up to an entire town, complete with homes, stables, church, school, town square, and streets.

Stripped of their weapons, Murphy, Ward, and Tyler were led into the camp on foot, having tied their horses to a post on the outside.

The leader of the camp, a man of about sixty named Glenndonna, met them at the town square at a long table where lunch was served.

The table held twenty people. Once Murphy, Ward, and Tyler took chairs next to Glenndonna, every chair was occupied.

"It is our custom to serve lunch at this table to visitors," Glenndonna said.

"We appreciate it," Ward said. "It was a long ride."

At the center of the table a man started to carve a large turkey.

"Now, what can I do for you, gentlemen?" Glenndonna asked politely.

"You can tell us about the family that was murdered on the road," Murphy said.

"Brother Titus was to be our new bishop," Glenndonna said. "Replacing Bishop Rand who recently passed away from old age and influenza."

"Where were they coming from?" Murphy asked.

"A settlement in Arizona."

"You buried them here?"

"We have our own cemetery."

"From the looks of things you have your own everything," Murphy said.

"We burden no one and ask the same in return."

"Mr. Glenndonna, I believe Mr. Titus and his family were killed by mistake," Murphy said.

"How do you shoot seven people by mistake?" Glenndonna asked.

"There have been dozens of settlers traveling west and as many railroad men killed by a sniper in the past three months," Murphy said.

"What takes place outside our walls is no concern of mine," Glenndonna said.

"I think the sniper mistook your bishop for a settler," Murphy said. "And if you plan to send for a new bishop, I would advise him not to travel looking like a settler or he could wind up the same way."

Glenndonna stared at Murphy for a moment.

"I'll take that under advisement," he said.

"You might notify the marshal when a new bishop is on the way so he can arrange protection," Murphy said.

"We deal with our own," Glenndonna said.

"Then you might have another murdered bishop on your hands."

Glenndonna nodded. "I'll take that under advisement as well."

"Good."

The man carving the turkey set a massive platter of turkey meat in front of Glenndonna.

"Let us pray and give thanks," Glenndonna said.

As Murphy and Ward walked along Main Street to the marshal's office, Murphy asked, "Where is the telegraph office?"

"Right around the corner from the railroad depot."

"I need to send a wire. I'd be obliged if you accompanied me."

"Afternoon, Marshal," the telegraph operator said.

"This is Mr. Murphy from Washington," Ward said. "He needs to send a wire."

The operator grabbed a paper and pencil.

"No, he needs to send it himself," Ward said. "I'll explain outside."

Once Ward and the operator were outside,

Murphy sat at the key and sent a message to Burke.

On my way to Philadelphia Stop Will explain upon arrival Stop Murphy

SEVENTEEN

Philadelphia was an enormous metropolis of almost nine hundred thousand people. Its history was rich; its importance in the founding of the country second to none, and its value to the nation as a port and industry leader invaluable.

So said the pamphlet Murphy read on the train as it rolled into Union Station.

He dumped the pamphlet into a garbage bin as he retrieved Boyle from the boxcar and led him away from the station to a large livery stable outside of the downtown area of the city.

Carrying firearms openly was prohibited inside the city limits so Murphy removed his gun belt and tucked it inside his satchel.

Then he caught a horse-driven taxi and told the driver to take him to the Sharps rifle factory at Mill Creek.

The drive took almost an hour and Murphy told the driver to wait for him and gave him twenty dollars on top of the fare to hold the carriage.

The factory was a large, very imposing one-story building surrounded by an iron gate and patrolled by armed security guards.

Murphy gave his identification to a guard at the gate and requested a meeting with the factory manager. After a thirty-minute wait, Murphy was escorted inside the massive building.

"I'm not sure what impresses me the most," factory manager Alfred Peet said. "That you're a congressman or a special investigator for the President."

"Either will do so long as we can talk," Murphy said.

They were in Peet's large, very cluttered office. Peet sat behind his desk. Murphy in a chair opposite the desk.

"Talk about what?" Peet asked.

"Your Sharps rifle."

"We make other rifles here besides the Sharps," Peet said. "And sadly production of the Sharps will come to an end in another year or so. More modern weapons are in demand by the military these days I'm afraid."

"I'm sorry to hear that," Murphy said. "I carried a Sharps proudly during the war. It never failed me."

"So how can I help you?" Peet asked.

"This is classified information and not to leave this office," Murphy said. "A sniper out west is using a Sharps rifle to assassinate railroad workers and settlers from very long distances with .50-90 ammunition."

".50-90, that's a buffalo round."

"I know."

"How long a distance?"

"Fifteen hundred yards."

"Fifteen . . . that's impossible."

"Not if he had a 34-inch barrel instead of the standard 30-inch."

Peet nodded. "That might be possible. What's the connection between the railroad workers and settlers?"

"I can't answer that at this time," Murphy said. "All I can tell you is he's damn good with a Sharps and I need to find him before he kills again."

"What do you need from me?"

"Can you find out how many were made with a 34-inch barrel, the serial numbers on them, and where they were shipped to?" Murphy asked. "Here and in your Connecticut factory."

"That will take some legwork."

"I know, but there can't be that many 34-inch barrels made during the past ten or twelve years," Murphy said.

"Like I said, it will take some time," Peet said. "Two, maybe three days to check orders here and in our Connecticut factory."

"Send me a telegram in Washington when you have the list," Murphy said. "I'll grab a train and pick it up in person."

"That won't be necessary, Mr. Murphy," Peet said. "I'll have it delivered by courier to your home."

"Thank you," Murphy said.

"Give your address to my girl at the desk outside," Peet said.

Murphy took Boyle for a ride in the open fields behind his home in Virginia. If he didn't run for two days, the powerful male grew restless in his stall and kicked up a fuss until Murphy strapped the saddle on him.

They rode the morning away and when they returned to the barn, Murphy gave Boyle carrots and sugar cubes while he brushed and groomed him.

As he walked back to the house, a carriage came down the road. Murphy waited for the carriage to arrive at the gate.

"Congressman Murphy?" the driver of the carriage asked.

"Yes."

"I have a package for you, Congressman."

The wood box weighed about twenty pounds. Murphy carried it into the house to the table in the kitchen. It was nailed shut and he used a claw hammer to remove the lid.

Directly on top was a large sealed envelope.

He removed the envelope and set it aside.

Below the envelope was the 34-inch barrel of a newly drilled Sharps rifle, the stock and assembly, a tool kit for assembling, and a box of one hundred rounds.

Murphy tore open the envelope. Inside was a handwritten list of serial numbers and locations of gun shops and general stores around the country.

Peet inscribed a note on the second page.

One hundred and three custom-made 34-inch barrel rifles produced between 1860 and 1880 in .50-90 ammunition. One hundred and four now. Good luck and good hunting. Andrew Peet.

Murphy lifted the heavy 34-inch-long barrel and stared down the front sights.

"Hello, old friend," he said, softly.

Ninety minutes later, Murphy carried the

fully assembled Sharps rifle to the barn and saddled Boyle. He grabbed a shovel with a straight handle, then placed the Sharps in the saddle sleeve and rode Boyle to the field behind the house.

Murphy rode a distance of about twelve hundred yards, dismounted, and stuck the handle of the shovel into the ground a foot deep so that it made a nice target to aim at in the afternoon sunlight.

He rode Boyle back to the barn and carried the Sharps to the edge of the field and searched for the shovel.

He spotted it and removed a .50-90 round from his pocket, opened the breech to load the round, and then closed it.

He flipped up the rear sights and then took careful aim at the shovel. He held his breath and squeezed the trigger.

The Sharps all but exploded with its power.

The shot missed the target.

Murphy reloaded, aimed, and missed the target once again.

He tested the wind by tossing some dirt in the air and adjusted the rear sight one click, then fed a third round into the chamber.

Aim.

Hold breath.

Freeze.

Squeeze.

Just like during the war.

Three seconds after he fired the third shot he heard the metallic clink of bullet striking iron.

Murphy fired ten more rounds at the target and heard the clink of bullet on metal ten more times.

He went to the barn for Boyle and rode out to the shovel.

There were ten dents in the iron from ten rounds finding their mark.

Over dinner Murphy read the list of locations the one hundred and three .50-90 rifles were delivered to. Most were ordered and shipped to buffalo country in the west. Only a select few were manufactured during the last two years.

Of course a rifle ordered in seventy-five could have sat on the shelf of a store gathering dust until some buffalo skinner wandered in and decided to pay the hefty price tag for the weapon and its ammunition.

Murphy stared at the list not seeing what he needed to see to make a connection.

He didn't want to visit every shop and store on the list to find out how many rifles were sold and to whom and how many still sat on the shelf.

But it was looking like he might have to in order to get the answer.

Murphy finished dinner and went to the barn. He lit a lantern and gave Boyle a carrot stick and then gave him a good brushing.

"Looks like we have more riding to do, Boyle," Murphy said as he ran the brush along Boyle's thick back.

Once Boyle's coat gleamed in the light from the lantern, he gave him another carrot stick, turned off the light, and returned to the house.

He filled a glass with his father's whiskey and sat with his pipe at the table in the kitchen and stared at the list.

Next to the list sat the box of one hundred rounds of .50-90 ammunition.

His eyes shifted to the box and then it clicked.

"Of course," Murphy said and tossed back his drink.

EIGHTEEN

The reply to the telegram Murphy sent to Andrew Peet came four hours after he sent it from the telegraph office on Capitol Hill.

While he waited, Murphy walked around the park and the Hill and took lunch at a restaurant where the senators and congress-men didn't gather.

By the time he returned to the telegraph office the reply was waiting in a sealed envelope. He took it to a bench in the park opposite the White House, stuffed and lit his pipe, and tore open the envelope.

To Murphy Stop Four cases of one hundred .50-90 ammunition ordered and shipped to gunsmith in Silver City, New Mexico, six months ago Stop Andrew Peet

Murphy was smoking his pipe on the bench when Burke exited the White House, passed through the gates, and entered the park. He sat on the bench next to Murphy.

"I'm certain John Quad ordered four cases of .50-90 Sharps ammunition at a gun store in Silver City, New Mexico," Murphy said.

Burke nodded. "Close to his farm."

"He went home," Murphy said.

"You'll go there?"

"In the morning."

"Good luck."

Murphy stood up from the bench.

"Remember there is to be no publicity and no trial," Burke said.

Murphy started walking away from the bench.

"Your country and President are grateful, Murphy," Burke said. "Remember that, too."

Silver City was located in the southwestern part of New Mexico about five hundred miles south of Santa Fe.

It was a good area of the state to hide in if one were seeking refuge. Not much there except surrounding desert and quick access to Arizona if the need arose and with many hiding out in the area, the need arose often.

Murphy left the railroad in Sacramento, New Mexico, and rode southwest for two days into Silver City. Made famous for the silver strike in 1870, and made even more famous when Billy the Kid was arrested there in 1875. A violent town, Murphy could see how a man like Quad could get lost in it.

Despite its reputation for violence and crime, the streets were full of pedestrians, including women and children, when Murphy entered town and rode along Main Street. He dismounted and tied Boyle to the post outside of the sheriff's office.

The sidewalk was an elevated wood plank. Murphy stepped up and grabbed the doorknob.

County Sheriff Kevin Langston, seated at his desk, looked up from his paperwork as Murphy entered the office.

"I must say that I don't like the looks of you," Langston said.

Murphy had his wallet out and lowered the identification on the desk.

Langston looked down at it and then up at Murphy.

"You're kidding," Langston said.

Murphy looked at the coffee pot resting on the woodstove in the corner of the office. "Is that hot?"

"Help yourself," Langston said.

There were tin cups on a shelf behind the stove and Murphy filled one and took it to a chair opposite the desk and sat.

"Are you aware of the multiple murders

happening inside of four states involving the railroad and new settlers?" Murphy asked.

"I'm a county sheriff," Langston said. "I'm aware. So far none have been committed inside my jurisdiction."

"Maybe, but I believe the weapon he is using to commit these crimes came from the gun shop in your town," Murphy said. "That makes it your jurisdiction."

"Quinn's place?" Langston said. "Are you sure?"

"I think so, yes. Care to walk over there with me? I have some questions he may not want to answer."

"Yeah, I remember him, Sheriff," Quinn said as he came out from behind the counter of his very large store. "That .50-90 sat on the shelf for years collecting dust. Some buffalo skinner ordered it back in seventy-six. Said he was going north to hunt buffalo, but was killed in a card game the day before it was delivered. That was before you came along."

"Never mind that now, Quinn," Langston said. "What about the fellow who bought the rifle and ammunition?"

"Like I said, this fellow rides in and says he wants to buy the Sharps rifle on the shelf," Quinn said. "I didn't have the ammunition for it because I never expected anybody to buy it. He said he'd wait if I ordered four cases of ammunition. I told him he needed to pay in advance on account of I don't want to get stuck again like with the buffalo skinner."

"He paid cash?" Murphy asked.

"Fifty for the rifle, forty for the ammunition."

"Paper or gold coin?"

"Paper."

"What did he look like?"

"Big son of a bitch," Quinn said. "As big or bigger than you. Had long hair, a thick beard, and I thought it odd at the time that he was dressed more like a cowboy than buffalo hunter, but he paid cash so I sold it to him. Why wouldn't I?"

"Was he packing a sidearm?"

"I think so, yeah," Quinn said. "A Schofield I believe."

"Was it worn on his right hip or left?"

Quinn paused to think for a moment. "Left."

"You're sure?"

Quinn nodded. "Only 'cause I don't see too many left-handed guns. It was definitely left."

Murphy nodded. "What about small talk?"

"Small talk?" Quinn said.

"Did he say where he was from, where he was going, what he needed the Sharps for, that kind of thing?"

"I don't recall," Quinn said. "He was kind of quiet like and I mind my own business if I can help it."

"What about his name?" Murphy asked.

"I don't . . . hold on, I have a copy of the bill of sale in my files."

Quinn went to his office in back of the store and returned a few minutes later with a copy of the bill of sale. "That new ink carbon paper," he said and handed the paper to Murphy.

Murphy read the name.

"John Smith," Murphy said. "Really?"

Quinn nodded. "That's what he wrote."

"One last question," Murphy said. "Has he ever been back?"

"Not to my store," Quinn said. "I can't speak for the town."

"What now?" Langston asked.

Murphy struck a match and lit his pipe.

"Back to Sacramento and north to Santa Fe," Murphy said. "I'm going to try and pick up his trail if I can."

"Let me ask you something," Langston said. "What makes a man kill like that? For no reason at all."

"He has a reason."

"What?"

"For whatever the cause, he's insane," Murphy said. "Feel like having dinner with me? I fancy a steak."

"What did you mean when you said he's insane?" Langston said. "How could he function, murder like this if he's insane?"

Murphy sliced off a piece of steak, put it in his mouth, chewed, and swallowed. "I've done some studying in medical books and on psychiatry. It's possible to be insane, but not crazy. What he's doing makes him insane, but he's far from being a madman. Just the opposite. He functions at a very high level."

"I'm just a sheriff of a small county in the middle of nowhere," Langston said. "I'm not sure if I know what you're talking about."

"The part of his mind that knows right from wrong no longer functions," Murphy said. "The part of his mind that controls his actions functions at a very high level. He's highly skilled in the art of sniper warfare and knows who he wants to kill, how, and where, but he no longer feels any right or wrong in what he's doing."

"I've always believed in good and bad,"

Langston said. "You make it sound as if in some way he's not responsible."

"The part of him that is insane is not," Murphy said.

"All right, say I buy that insane business," Langston said. "He still needs a reason to kill innocent men, women, and children."

"In his mind he has the best reason of all," Murphy said. "Revenge."

The room at the Sacramento Hotel was cramped and dry and Murphy spent a restless night in a too soft bed.

When he walked into the small, Idaho church his intent was to kill in cold blood the last of the men that murdered his wife and child.

There was no mercy in his soul that Sunday morning. Hiding in a church does not absolve you of your crimes and erase the sins of your past.

Only God could do that.

And Murphy wasn't God.

He felt the eyes upon him as he entered the church and walked down the center aisle. He heard the whispers and gasps as people saw the cocked pistol in his hand. And when he shot the man in the back of the head the whispers and gasps became screams of terror that echoed in his ears as he walked out of the church and rode out of town.

Murphy's eyes snapped open in the dark hotel room.

He face was drenched in sweat.

His heart was beating like a scared rabbit.

He sat up in bed, struck a match, and lit the oil lamp on the table beside the bed.

Then he stood and dug the bottle of his father's whiskey out of his satchel. He filled a water glass from the dresser and as he sipped, he looked into the mirror.

"My God," Murphy said aloud. "We're both the same."

NINETEEN

Johnson met Murphy when he got off the connector train at the Santa Fe railroad camp. Murphy had taken the train in Sacramento, New Mexico, to the town of Santa Fe and then rode the special train that traveled from town to camp.

"I didn't think I would see you again so soon, if ever," Johnson said.

Walking Boyle to the hitching post outside Johnson's private train, Murphy asked, "Is your surveyor in camp?"

"He's taken ill I'm afraid," Johnson said. "His replacement is due in the morning. Why?"

"I have a rather large favor to ask," Murphy said.

"Can you ask it over dinner?" Johnson said. "Moy is making sliced chicken strips in sauce with rice and vegetables."

"I want to check the land surrounding the

railroad route of the westward Santa Fe line near the town of Shayville," Murphy said.

"Whatever for?" Johnson asked.

"The man I'm after once lived there."

"You mean the assassin?"

"Yes."

"We're ahead of schedule at this point," Johnson said. "The men are working sundown to sunup and we should connect to Dodge camp in twenty days. I suppose I could spare our surveyor for a few days."

"Good."

"I suppose the camp can spare me for a few days if you'd allow me to tag along."

"I don't see that as a problem."

"Good. So you'll spend the night in the guest room here?"

"I will, but we need to leave as soon as your surveyor arrives," Murphy said. "We need to stop at Sacramento to check records at the land office to look at a deed."

"I expect him to arrive at eight in the morning on a special run," Johnson said. "We'll do an immediate turnaround."

Moy entered the dining car with a rolling trolley filled with plates and bowls of steaming hot food.

"Can Moy make the trip?" Murphy said. "I really do enjoy his food."

■ ■ ■ ■

Milford Cook was quite put out at being shuffled onto Johnson's private train and taken to Sacramento the moment he arrived at the Santa Fe camp. A veteran of twenty plus years as a railroad land surveyor he carried a heavy stick with the home office and would not be treated like a servant by a chief camp engineer.

"I'm here to do a job and that job consists of accurately measuring distance and land and to save the board of directors' money and not to take whimsical rides in your private car," Cook said to Johnson.

Murphy entered Johnson's car as Cook finished speaking.

Cook stood all of five-foot-four inches tall in his boots and looked up at Murphy, who towered over him.

"That whimsical ride you spoke of wasn't a request," Murphy said. "Can you ride a horse?"

Cook all but gulped. "No."

"Then we'll rent you a buggy."

Moy served a wonderful breakfast of scrambled eggs with tea cakes and tea that went a long way to soothing Cook's ruffled feathers.

Murphy explained the necessity of the trip to Cook while they ate.

"I suppose if I assist you in capturing this plague on the railroad, it will be a nice feather in my cap to the board," Cook said.

"How nice for you," Murphy said. "Mr. Johnson, we won't reach Sacramento for another three hours. I'll be in your spare bedroom taking a nap."

Late in the afternoon, Murphy, Johnson, and Cook left the county hall of records and deeds with an accurate map of the land where Quad's farm once stood and the route taken west by the railroad.

"We'll stay at the hotel in town and leave early in the morning," Murphy said. "If I read the maps correctly we have about a four-hour ride ahead of us."

Murphy packed supplies into the rented buggy and then mounted Boyle. Johnson, atop his own horse, looked at Cook.

"Are you ready, Mr. Cook?" Johnson asked.

Holding a short whip, Cook nodded. "I believe so, yes."

"Then let's go," Murphy said. "We'll follow the tracks, but you tell us when we reach the site where the Quad house once stood."

Part of the ride was pretty country. A great deal of it was desolate, almost desert in appearance. After two hours they rested the horses and gave them some water and grain. After another hour's ride the land evolved into lush green pastures and farmland except there wasn't a farmhouse in sight.

Murphy and Johnson rode slightly ahead of Cook's buggy.

"Mr. Johnson, Mr. Murphy, please hold for a moment," Cook said.

They turned and rode back to Cook.

"I believe we are here," Cook said. "I'll get my instruments and check the maps."

Murphy and Johnson helped Cook carry his leveling and theodolite to the field. Cook spent thirty minutes reading the maps and coordinating his measurements and then announced, "There. Three hundred yards to the northwest is where the house, barn, and corral once stood."

Cook pointed to a gently sloping hill a

hundred yards away. "On the other side of that hill where the tracks are used to be eighty acres of his farmland."

"Are you sure?" Johnson said.

"I've checked my readings three times. I'm sure."

Murphy mounted Boyle and rode to the field where John Quad and his family once lived. Johnson and Cook followed.

"They needed this land for the railroad," Murphy said. "But a dozen years ago that backland was farmland."

Murphy looked at the overgrown field where a house once stood. He turned and looked at the hills where Quad hid and waited for the Army and railroad people to show up.

"The house burned right here," Murphy said. "With Quad's wife and child hiding in the root cellar."

Johnson and Cook looked at the vacant, overgrown field.

"They died from smoke before the fire cremated them in the cellar," Murphy said.

Murphy closed his eyes.

"Quad killed a half dozen or more soldiers and railroad men that day they came to take his farm," Murphy said. "He lost his family, his farm, and then his freedom and all for . . ."

In the distance a train whistle blew.

Murphy opened his eyes and turned around. He couldn't see the train from where he stood, only the thick smoke from its stack as it moved along was visible.

"That," Murphy said.

Murphy built a campfire in the field and prepared a lunch of bacon, beans, fresh slices of beef from the store in town, paper-wrapped cornbread, and coffee.

"Twelve years of hard labor will play on a man's mind after he's lost everything he's cared about in this world, no doubt," Johnson said.

"I can understand his hatred for the railroad, but why attack innocent settlers?" Cook asked.

"His mind crossed over the edge," Murphy said. "All he sees is his hatred and need for revenge. Against the railroad for what it did to him. Against the settlers because he once was one and it cost him everything."

"He's insane," Cook said.

Murphy dug the bottle of his father's whiskey out of a saddlebag and added an ounce to each coffee cup.

"Maybe he's insane, but that doesn't mean he isn't smart and highly skilled," Murphy said. "And harder to catch than a greased pig in a mud pen."

Murphy sipped some coffee.

He looked at the hills where Quad once hid.

That could have been me, Murphy thought.

TWENTY

It was well after dark when Johnson's private train rolled into the Santa Fe railroad camp. Since the men were working in reverse, the camp was all but deserted except for a few railroad police, mess hall cooks, and the whores' tent.

Moy prepared a late supper in Johnson's dining car.

"We should connect the two camps inside of three weeks barring no setbacks," Johnson said.

"I'll make sure there aren't any," Cook said. "Tomorrow I'll survey the land for the final twenty miles and make any necessary adjustments. Do you have a buggy I can use?"

"No, but we do have some gentle horses to ride. I'll go with you," Johnson said.

Cook nodded. "What about you, Mr. Murphy?"

"I'll stop by the Dodge camp in the morning and then head into Dodge City," Murphy said.

"Then we'll leave together," Johnson said.

The pain from loss never really goes away. Like the thin skin of a freshly healed cut the skin could open and bleed at the slightest scratch. That's the way it was with the mental pain of losing your family and everything you loved.

More than fifteen years had passed since the murder of his wife and child and he had buried the pain and emotions deep, but they were always there waiting for the opportunity to arise and bleed.

Pain mixed with guilt was enough to drive a man insane.

The pain from the loss.

Guilt at having been the cause of it.

Worse when you hated being behind a plow so badly you risked your life to fight a war to get away from it.

His reason for moving to Washington was simple. Staying home or near home kept the wound open.

So now you are inside his head and know the reason for Quad's rampage. It is the same as your own.

How do you find him in a million square miles of open country?

Murphy was in a chair opposite the bed in Johnson's extra bedroom on his train. He had a glass of his father's whiskey to ease the anguish that threatened to bubble up inside his chest and consume him.

He finished the glass and drank two more and when the numbness set in he was ready for sleep.

Murphy retrieved Boyle from the boxcar on Johnson's private train. Johnson had his own horse and a tame filly for Cook alongside Boyle.

"You should make the Dodge camp by nightfall," Johnson said.

"Will you be back, Mr. Murphy?" Cook asked.

"Don't know," Murphy said. "I go where the evidence takes me."

Murphy mounted Boyle and with a gentle yank on the reins, he rode away toward the Dodge camp.

Close to nightfall Murphy rode by the train filled with workers and supplies for the night's work of laying tracks.

After dark, he entered the Dodge City railroad camp. Except for police on patrol, the camp was quiet with lanterns lighting the avenues between tents and makeshift buildings.

Bradley's private car was dark. He was probably with the men on the work train.

Sally Orr's large tent was closed and dark. With the men working nights there was not much for the whores to do except wait for morning.

Murphy tied Boyle to a post and walked down the rows of tents to Sally's large, private tent where she kept residence.

A light from inside shone through the canvas sides.

"Sally," Murphy said at the closed tent flap.

He could see her shadow on the inside move from bed to the flap and then it opened and she looked at him.

Murphy spoke softly. "May I come in?"

"Only if you promise to stay the night," Sally said.

Under the covers they waited for their breathing to return to normal. When it had, Sally reached for one of her thin cigars and lit it with the flame of the lantern beside the bed.

She blew a smoke ring.

"I got under your skin, cowboy," she said. "I can tell by the way you made love to me, I got under your skin."

"I don't deny that," Murphy said. "It's why I came back."

Sally puffed on the cigar and exhaled smoke through her nose. "So now what?"

"I don't know."

"You're still after that murderer?"

"Yes."

"And when you catch him, then what? Do you return to Washington and forget me, or do you come back to my arms?"

"I haven't thought that far ahead."

"Yes, you have. You wouldn't be in my bed otherwise."

Murphy sat up in bed. "I could use a drink."

"The bottle is on the dresser. Make it two."

Murphy stood and walked to the dresser and filled two water glasses with his father's whiskey and carried them to the bed.

"I see you're still drinking the good stuff," he said as he handed Sally a glass.

"I'm a good stuff kind of woman," Sally said.

Murphy sat and sipped from his glass.

Sally puffed on her cigar and sipped from her glass.

"I need a man in my life, Murphy, and you need a woman," Sally said. "We're both broken, I know that, but together we make

218

a nice fit. I can't make you forget what happened to your wife any more than you can erase my childhood, but does it matter at this point? What happened in the past doesn't have to destroy the present or the future."

"Will you keep the whorehouse in Saint Louis?" Murphy asked.

"I'm a madam. I don't whore," Sally said. "And unless you know another way I can earn a thousand a month you let me know."

"I have quite a bit stashed away," Murphy said.

"I said I need a man in my life," Sally said. "But, not as a banker. I'll share my bed with you, but I can support myself just fine."

"So how does this work?" Murphy asked.

"Well, I ain't moving to Washington," Sally said.

Murphy sipped from his glass and nodded. "When do you go back to Saint Louis?"

"As soon as the railroad is connected," Sally said. "Three weeks or so, no more than that."

"I'm used to being alone," Murphy said.

"Me, too. So what? Nothing and nobody gets to stay the same forever."

"All right, but first I have to finish what I started."

"I know that."

Sally set her drink on the table and patted the bed.

"Let's get some sleep," she said. "Or something."

Murphy set his glass next to Sally's. "Or something sounds better."

Murphy and Sally took breakfast in her tent shortly after the men arrived from work. The noise, laughter, and hustle of a hundred and fifty hungry men filtered into the tent even with the flaps closed.

From outside the tent, Bradley said, "Sally, is Mr. Murphy in there with you?"

"We're having breakfast," Sally said. "Come in."

Bradley opened the flap and stepped inside the tent.

"I saw your horse," he said. "I'm surprised to see you back so soon."

"I need a ride to Dodge," Murphy said.

"I'll have my engineer ready my car. You can leave within the hour."

"Thank you," Murphy said.

Bradley nodded and left the tent.

Sally glared at Murphy. "You're in one big Goddamn hurry."

"I have to finish this," Murphy said.

"So you just popped in for a quick fucking and pop out, is that how this is going to

220

work?" Sally said.

"That isn't true," Murphy said. "I told you I have to finish this. I never said otherwise."

"Well, go on then and get yourself killed, you big fool," Sally said.

"What about Saint . . ."

"Just go," Sally said. "Go on, get out."

Murphy stared at Sally.

"You heard me, get out," Sally said.

Murphy stood from the table, walked to the tent flap, opened it, and stepped out of the tent.

Sally wiped her eyes on a napkin. "Oh, Goddamn it," she whispered.

Murphy stepped down from the boxcar after loading Boyle and was surprised to see Sally standing beside Bradley's private riding car.

He walked to her.

"I thought you said . . ."

"Never mind what I said, you big idiot," Sally said. "If you don't show up in Saint Louis when you're done with this, I will hire a team of Pinkerton detectives to hunt you down and drag you there. Am I understood?"

"Yes."

"Then kiss me and go to work."

■ ■ ■ ■

Bradley and Murphy shook hands at the Dodge City railroad depot and then Murphy stepped down from the private car to retrieve Boyle.

He walked Boyle into town and along Main Street to Marshal Poule's office.

Poule was behind his desk when Murphy entered.

"I didn't figure to see you back this way so soon," Poule said.

"I need to send a wire," Murphy said. "Then I thought you might join me for lunch."

While Olson, the Dodge City telegraph operator, waited outside with Poule, Murphy sat at the desk and tapped out his message on the key using the secret code for Burke.

To William Burke the White House Stop Murphy coming to Washington in three days Stop Gather all records and information of the family of John Quad Stop Meet me at the station in Washington Stop Do not reply Stop Murphy

"Is that a Sharps rifle in your saddle?" Poule asked as he and Murphy walked to the

Dodge Hotel for lunch.

"A gift from the factory," Murphy said.

In front of the hotel, Murphy removed the Sharps and Winchester rifles from the saddle and took them inside to the dining room.

They ordered steak.

"Have there been any new shootings?" Poule asked as they ate.

"Just some Mormons I think he mistook for settlers."

"Mormons? Was Marshal Ward involved?"

"You know him?"

"He's a good man."

Murphy nodded as he sliced off a piece of steak.

"Why do you say mistook for settlers?"

"A Mormon bishop and his family traveling to Provo on the prairie in a covered wagon," Murphy said. "They looked like settlers to him and he eliminated them as he did the others."

"Children?"

"Five."

"Jesus."

Murphy ate a piece of steak and washed it down with a sip of coffee.

"What's his total, about a hundred dead?"

"I haven't done the math, but that sounds about right."

"And you're still on his trail alone?"

"I don't think a large posse or detachment from the Army can catch him," Murphy said. "He knows how to avoid them, move at night, and keep his distance. For him this is a war and we trained him how to fight it."

"So where are you going now?"

"Washington. Sometimes you have to fight a war from a desk."

Murphy filled a water glass with his father's whiskey, lit his pipe, and sat in the chair in his hotel room. The bottle was close to empty. He would have to remember to pack an extra bottle or two when he headed out again.

He pulled his watch out of the watch pocket on his vest and held it in his hand. It was solid silver with a decorative face cover. He pushed the stem down and the cover plate snapped open. The time read ten past ten. He gave the stem a few winds then closed the face plate.

He turned the watch around to the back plate. It was decorated as was the front. There was a slight indentation at the top and he used a fingernail to open the back cover plate.

The smiling face of his wife adorned the

interior of the back plate. In sixty-four, his wife took a trip to Memphis to have the watch made for him at a cost of forty dollars because of the silver. Then she hired a portrait artist to paint her image on the back cover plate and mailed him the watch for his birthday.

Less than a month later she and their son would be dead.

She'd been gone more than fifteen years and somehow it seemed like only yesterday. After he killed the last of them in the church he stopped referring to Katherine by name and called her his wife.

Somehow that made it easier to swallow the pain.

Murphy wondered what John Quad called his wife.

Murphy stared at the tiny painting of Katherine.

"I'm sorry, Katherine, but once I've finished this business with Quad it's time to move on with my life," he said and closed the back cover plate.

TWENTY-ONE

Burke waited for Murphy to lead his horse out of the depot to the waiting area where his buggy lined the street with a dozen others.

"Did you bring the information I requested?" Murphy asked.

"In my buggy."

"Follow me home. I'll need to stop at the market on the way."

"I already did that," Burke said. "I also brought a change of clothes."

"Then I'll give Boyle's back a rest and ride in the buggy with you," Murphy said and tied the horse to the rear of the buggy.

Burke had done a thorough job researching the family history of John Quad. His parents died in the influenza outbreak in Ohio in seventy-seven before his release from prison.

His only sibling, a younger sister by three years named Reeva, married a Swede named

Jorgen Bensen in sixty-nine and migrated west to Colorado, near Colorado Springs, close to the Rocky Mountains.

They operated a large general store for trappers, settlers, and the general population. They had three children, a son and two daughters. They had a fourth who died of pneumonia shortly after birth.

After dinner Murphy broke out his detailed map of the area. From Colorado Springs, Quad had easy access to New Mexico, Kansas, Utah, and Arizona by horse and railroad.

"What happened to the family farm in Ohio?" Murphy said.

"It was left in a will to the daughter," Burke said. "As far as we can tell, it sits unworked."

Murphy looked at the map again. "I'll be going here," he said and placed his finger over Colorado Springs.

Burke looked at the map and nodded.

After Burke retired to the guest room, Murphy took his gear to the den along with several cleaning kits.

He lit several oil lanterns on the desk to provide as much light as possible.

He broke down the Schofield .45 and removed all working parts and screws. After a thorough cleaning with a wire brush, he oiled and reassembled the handgun with new screws from the cleaning kit. He loaded six rounds into the wheel, closed the top break, and inserted the .45 into his holster.

Murphy set the Henry rifle aside, opting to bring just the Winchester and Sharps.

Although the Henry rifle was no longer produced after the war, Murphy kept the weapon for sentimental reasons rather than for functionality.

He broke down the Winchester and cleaned and oiled all parts and replaced worn screws with new ones from the kit. Once fully loaded he inserted fifteen rounds into the tubular magazine and set it aside.

He took special care with the Sharps rifle, breaking it down, oiling all parts, reassembling it slowly and carefully. He wore a double-sided bandolero during the war that held twelve rounds of .50-90 on each side. The leather was faded and worn, but he greased and polished it and then fed twenty-four rounds into the slots.

He removed the knife sheath from his holster. The knife was a standard field knife used by hunters and trappers everywhere and had an eight-inch-long single-edge blade. He set it aside and removed the Bowie knife from the bottom desk drawer.

The blade of the knife was fifteen inches long with a curved tip. Jim Bowie created the knife for only one reason, for close fighting. The knife was more a short sword than a practical field knife.

Murphy felt the blade. He used a sharpening stone to hone the edge to razor sharp. Then he replaced the knife in the sheath and attached it to his holster.

Satisfied with his gear, Murphy retired to his bedroom. He poured a drink of his father's whiskey and smoked his pipe and waited for the need to sleep to overcome him.

Burke was drinking coffee in the kitchen when Murphy joined him. For a moment, Burke was startled by Murphy's appearance. Dressed in a suit with tie, a long frock coat, and polished boots, Murphy more resembled a Sunday school teacher than trained sniper and man hunter.

"I almost forgot that you are taking the train this morning," Burke said.

"If you mean my clothing, I find it easier to travel dressed this way and change when I arrive at my destination," Murphy said. "So I don't upset passengers and the conductor."

"I'll ride in with you to the station right

after we have some breakfast," Burke said.

Murphy loaded Boyle into the boxcar and then walked to the front of the train where Burke waited beside his buggy.

"How are you on expense money?" Burke asked.

"Barely made a dent," Murphy said as he removed his large satchel from the buggy.

"Wire if you need more."

"I will."

"How long do you figure to be gone?"

"Until the job is done."

Burke extended his right hand to Murphy and they shook.

"Good luck," Burke said.

Murphy nodded.

"Thanks," he said and boarded the train.

Twenty-Two

After three days and nights on the train, Murphy checked into the small hotel near the railroad in Denver, Colorado. He put Boyle up in the livery beside the hotel. In the morning he would make the trip south to Colorado Springs, figuring on three days in the saddle.

Tonight he wanted nothing more than a hot bath, a shave, a decent dinner, and a good night's sleep. He got all four at the surprisingly comfortable hotel for a modest fee.

In the morning he changed into black trail clothes and strapped on his holster and bandolero and went for breakfast in the hotel dining room.

After breakfast, he saddled Boyle, purchased supplies for the trip at the general store near the hotel, and began the ride south to Colorado Springs.

He rode until sunset and made camp.

Around a fire he ate a light supper of beans, bacon, and biscuits from the general store and drank coffee sweetened from a new bottle of his father's whiskey.

Although it was late spring, he was at a high altitude and the winds blowing east from the Rockies had a chill in them. He fed the fire and got into the bedroll and closed his eyes and mind to thought.

The job that waited for him was not for the faint of heart or the distracted.

There wasn't room for thoughts of Sally or Katherine or anything else that might sway his vision from the target. It wasn't much different than the war. A sniper in enemy territory had to keep his wits about him at all times and sleep with one eye open when he got the chance to sleep.

Except this wasn't the war and he wasn't a young man escaping from behind a plow. The years of isolation and loneliness had taken their toll on his spirit. Sally had awakened something in him that he thought was lost forever and . . .

He was doing the very thing he needed to avoid.

Think.

He shut out thoughts of Sally and willed his mind blank and for sleep to take him to morning.

■ ■ ■ ■

Murphy reached the edge of Colorado Springs mid-morning of the third day in the saddle. The air was thin at over a mile high and chilled from winds whipping down off Pikes Peak in the background.

At over 14,000 feet above sea level, the peak still had pockets of snow on top that probably never melted.

Murphy paused to look at the Rocky Mountains, which dominated the background. Beautiful and deadly, many a trapper, hunter, and panhandler ventured up there never to return below.

A half mile in front of him Murphy could see the large general store at the base of the hills about one-half mile away from town. Smoke rose up from a tall chimney and from a distance seemed to mingle with the white clouds overhead. There was no sign of a house on either side of the store. Either the Bensen family lived above or behind the store or had a house elsewhere. He rode directly to the store and dismounted. The store was large, maybe forty feet long with a large handpainted sign above the door. *Bensen's General Store and Mercantile.*

Horses and wagons were tied to several

hitching posts at the base of the long wooden porch. Racks of goods lined the porch and several women browsed through clothing and housewares.

As Murphy climbed the steps to the porch, he drew stares from several women browsing goods.

He pushed through the swinging doors and entered the first of three rooms that made up the interior of the store.

A woman was behind a long counter. She was operating a hand-cranked till to ring up the sale of a dress a woman customer was buying.

Murphy browsed the room. Goods were a mixture of men's and women's clothing, barrels of food, dry goods such as flour and sugar, tools, housewares, a catalogue counter, and even school books and supplies.

He wandered into the second room where a group of men were shopping farm implements and tools. The third room housed specialty items such as furniture, Franklin woodstoves, music boxes, and other such luxury items.

In the third room he spotted a closed door and walked to it. He grabbed the doorknob and was about to turn it when a man walked up beside him.

"That's not part of the store, friend," the man said with a slight Swedish accent.

"I thought it was another room of goods," Murphy said.

"What you see is what you get," the man said. "That door is private. I'm Jorgen Bensen, owner of this establishment."

"Murphy."

"Mr. Murphy, is there something I can help you find?"

"Supplies. Food, mostly."

"Taking a trip into the mountains to try your hand at gold?"

"Thinking about it."

"Pick out what you need," Bensen said. "My wife will ring you up at the counter."

"The woman working that cash machine?"

"My wife, Reeva," Bensen said. "That machine came all the way from Chicago. It's the latest invention for keeping track of transactions."

Murphy nodded. "I'll pick out my goods."

A while later Murphy carried a sack of flour, coffee, and beans to the counter. He waited for the woman in front of him to pay for a dress and then he said, "I'd like five pounds of jerky, bacon, a pound of sugar and condensed milk, and some canned fruit if you got it. And a pouch of pipe tobacco."

"I have peaches and pears in cans," Reeva said.

"That will do."

Reeva added the transaction on the cash machine and rang up a total.

"That will be eleven dollars even," she said.

Murphy dug out his wallet and counted out eleven dollars.

"Want it wrapped in paper?"

"Sure."

As Reeva wrapped the goods, Murphy browsed the jars of candy under glass.

"Let me get a few of those candy sticks there in that jar."

Reeva removed a few sticks from the jar and handed them to Murphy.

"That will be a nickel."

Murphy carried the wrapped sacks outside to Boyle and stuffed them into oversized saddlebags.

He mounted Boyle and rode west of the general store until he was behind it, and studied the rear of the building.

They lived in a home attached to the store by the door he tried to open.

Murphy camped a half mile behind the Bensen General Store and waited for night. He made a campfire and fixed a quick meal of bacon with beans and coffee and afterward sucked on a candy stick.

After eating he extinguished the fire and drank coffee sweetened with a touch of his father's whiskey. Then he lit his pipe and watched the dark horizon in front of him until he saw lights come on in the Bensen home.

The day was done, the store was closed, and the family was in their home for the evening meal.

Murphy finished the pot of coffee and smoked two bowls in his pipe while he waited for the Bensen family to settle in for the night.

One by one the lanterns went out in windows. He waited another hour for the moon to rise and then saddled Boyle and rode to within a hundred feet of the Bensen home and dismounted. He walked Boyle around to the front of the store and tied him to a hitching post.

He removed his boots and climbed the stairs to the porch in his stocking feet. The racks of goods that lined the porch earlier were gone. He tried the door behind the swinging doors and it was locked.

He walked the length of the porch on both ends and the windows were shut and locked, except one, the window behind the counter where the cash register machine was located.

He withdrew the Bowie knife from its sheath and slid it between window and ledge and slowly opened the window wide enough for him to fit through. He replaced the knife, reached for the ledge, and quietly pulled himself up and over the open window and behind the counter.

The interior of the store was dark and moonlight was the only illumination. He stood behind the counter and waited for his night vision to adjust, a trick he had learned as a sniper in the war.

When his eyes were fully adjusted Murphy slowly walked across the wood floor in his stocking feet to the door that led to the house. It wasn't locked. He quietly opened the door and entered the home.

Heat from a crackling fire in the fireplace hit him in the face as he stepped into the living room. The added light from the fire illuminated a hallway to the left and another to the right of the fireplace.

Murphy crept down the left hallway where there were two doors.

Bedrooms.

One for the boy, the other shared by the sisters.

Murphy opened the first door. The boy

was asleep in his bed. Murphy walked to the bed and placed his hand over the boy's mouth and he bolted awake and tried to sit up.

"Easy, boy," Murphy said. "I'm not here to hurt you. I'm just here to talk to your ma and pa. Let's go."

Murphy held his hand over the boy's mouth as he walked back to the living room and down the other hallway to the master bedroom. He withdrew the Bowie knife, flipped it around so the dull side was against the boy's neck, and used his right foot to crash in the door.

Jorgen Bensen and Reeva jumped up from bed at the sound of the crash. Jorgen reached for a shotgun that rested against the wall beside the nightstand.

"Don't do that," Murphy said.

Reeva looked at her son and gasped.

Jorgen lowered his hands and looked at Murphy.

"What do you want?" Jorgen asked. "Money?"

"Talk," Murphy said. "Just to talk."

"I'd believe you a lot better if you released my son," Jorgen said.

Murphy released the boy and he ran to Reeva.

"Mrs. Bensen, why don't you make us a

pot of coffee," Murphy said.

"I can't believe my brother has done the things that you say," Reeva commented.

"Can I have another slice of apple pie, Ma?" the boy asked.

"A small one and take it with you back to bed," Reeva said. "And don't leave any crumbs in the bed," she added.

"Why didn't you state your business earlier when you were in the store," Jorgen asked.

"The element of surprise is an attention getter," Murphy said. "Had I spoken to your wife about her brother in the store she would have called me a liar and thrown me out. At least now you are listening to me."

"That doesn't mean I believe you," Reeva said.

"He's a big man, your brother," Murphy said. "As tall or taller than I. He's left-handed and an expert marksman from his days as an Army sniper. He spent twelve years in a federal prison for a crime that never should have happened in the first place. He blames the railroad and holds a grudge against the government settlement program for the death of his wife and child, and to be honest I don't blame him for that. However, his grudge has driven him insane and innocent men, women, and children are being murdered by his hand."

"My brother would never harm a child," Reeva said.

"Your brother wouldn't, but John Quad is no longer the brother you once knew," Murphy said. "His troubles have driven him mad and that madness can't control his need for revenge."

Jorgen shook his head as he looked at Reeva.

"I believe him, honey," he said. "I've heard the talk, read the newspaper stories, and the government wouldn't send Mr. Murphy all the way out here unless there was just cause to do so."

Reeva wiped tears from her eyes and nodded.

"When was he last here?" Murphy asked.

"Ten days ago," Reeva said. "He needed supplies."

"Where did he go?"

"Into the mountains."

Murphy nodded and picked up his coffee cup.

"You'll be going after him then?" Jorgen said.

"Yes."

"He knows the mountains," Jorgen said. "And how to survive in them."

Reeva looked at Murphy with mist in her eyes. "Will you kill him?"

"Not if I can help it."

"You'll need a warmer coat," Jorgen said. "It may be late spring down here, but higher up toward the peaks, it can feel like winter in January."

"I'll pay you for one," Murphy said. "And gloves and a hat."

"Mr. Murphy, if you capture John alive, what will happen to him?" Reeva asked. "Will he go back to prison?"

"I would say that he will spend the rest of his life in a hospital," Murphy said.

"For the insane," Reeva said.

"I'm sorry to say that would be true, but a hospital for the insane is a far better place than a maximum federal prison for the sane," Murphy said.

Reeva nodded.

"You'll need a warmer blanket for your horse," Jorgen said. "Let's go into the store."

Jorgen selected a coat made from bear skin, a hat from beaver and gloves woven of wool, and a heavy wool blanket for Boyle.

"How much for all of that?" Murphy asked.

"I don't want your money," Reeva said.

"What I want is your promise that if at all possible, you will take John alive."

"I will do my best not to kill him," Murphy said. "That's not a promise, but it's the best I can offer."

Reeva nodded.

Murphy gathered up his new coat and accessories. He was about to leave the store, then paused to turn around.

"It might be a good idea to get a good watchdog for the store," Murphy said. "You have a family to protect."

Twenty-Three

Murphy rode Boyle to the base of Pikes Peak where he dismounted and decided to make camp for the night. There was an hour of daylight left and he didn't want to risk Boyle tripping in the dark and breaking a leg.

The base of the mountains was a mile or more above sea level and the chilled winds blowing down from the top made it feel more like March than late spring. He made a fire and covered Boyle with the extra blanket and then hobbled him close to the fire to keep him warm overnight.

He fixed bacon, beans, and jerky with coffee for supper and treated himself to a can of peaches afterward.

With his saddlebags as a pillow, Murphy got into his bedroll and watched as the moon rose to illuminate the mountains.

Being from Tennessee, Murphy knew the mountains and how deadly they could be to man and animal. Underestimating them even in summer was a mistake many a man made only once as they rarely gave a second chance.

Quad had a ten-day head start and there was no guarantee he was still up there. He could be long gone and on his way to the site of his next rampage.

It was a chance he had to take to pick up his trail.

A trail that could lead to anywhere.

How far did he want to go to end this?

Murphy felt his eyes grow heavy. Even though the Sharps and Winchester were at arm's length, he pulled the .45 from the holster and kept it in the bedroll with him.

After breakfast, Murphy saddled Boyle and then rode slowly toward the incline that led to Pikes Peak.

He dismounted and smoked his pipe as he studied the majestic mountain.

He had no idea the course Quad followed into the mountains.

Quad could have followed any trail to any mountain, why pick the tallest, most treacherous one to ascend into hiding?

If indeed his goal was to hide.

Quad could be using the time to regroup and select his next site for a massacre.

And that could be anywhere a settler is moving to or any railroad extension under construction.

Murphy rubbed Boyle's neck. "Well, as Ben Franklin proved that lightning always takes the path of the least resistance I think we should do the same," he said.

Murphy mounted Boyle and chose the kindest, smoothest path up the mountain for a thousand feet. The trek took most of the morning.

He dismounted and rested Boyle for a bit, feeding him a carrot stick and sugar cubes.

While Boyle rested, Murphy ate a jerky stick and took a few sips of water.

Then he brushed Boyle's coat.

"The thing you never want to do is work up a sweat while riding into cold weather," Murphy said. "A sweat is a death sentence in the cold. Remember that."

Taking the reins, Murphy led Boyle along a flat ridge and to higher ground. By late afternoon they had traveled another thousand feet and Murphy searched for flat ground to make camp.

As he removed the saddle from Boyle and brushed his coat, Murphy said, "No sign of him yet, boy. Maybe he chose another peak. Or maybe his sister told us a lie to cover up for him? We shall see tomorrow."

Gathering as much wood as possible, Murphy built a large campfire and fixed a quick meal. He fed Boyle oats and carrot sticks and then draped the heavier wool blanket around his back and covered that with the lighter saddle blanket.

"The sun is barely down and it's already getting cold," Murphy said as he hobbled Boyle near the fire.

Once he was satisfied Boyle was comfortable, Murphy spread his bedroll near the fire and settled in for the night.

A million stars twinkled overhead.

The moon illuminated silver clouds in the sky.

"God's country," Murphy said aloud and closed his eyes.

The crack of a rifle shot bolted Murphy awake. He grabbed the .45 and jumped to his feet as the echo of the shot faded into the mountains.

He stood perfectly still.

Waiting.

.45 at the ready.

A second shot fired and Murphy turned to face the source of the shot as it echoed throughout the mountains.

Boyle, hobbled, snorted his displeasure at the noise.

"It's all right, boy," Murphy said as he holstered the .45. "It's probably just a man hunting game."

The shot was a Sharps rifle bullet, of that Murphy had no doubt. He would recognize its distinctive sound anywhere. He put the distance, judging from the echo, at about a mile to the west.

On foot that was a two-day hike up the peak to the west.

As he removed the leather strips from Boyle's legs, Murphy said, "We best get started then. Right after breakfast."

An hour before sunset, Murphy led Boyle to the peak of the mountain where there was lush flat land mixed in with treacherous slopes and cliffs.

The air was thin. Boyle needed to adjust to the shallower breathing.

"By tomorrow you won't even notice the thin air," Murphy said as he removed the saddle from Boyle's back.

As he brushed Boyle's coat, Murphy spotted the buzzards flying high above the mountain a mile or more to the west.

"See them buzzards?" Murphy said. "That's our map. Tomorrow we'll go see what they're picking at."

Murphy hobbled Boyle beside a pine tree, removed the Winchester rifle from the saddle, and followed a path around the mountain to a large boulder that he used for cover.

Buzzards were picking at the remains of an elk kill. Entrails and stomach and there wasn't much left.

Murphy came out from behind the boulder and walked to the remains. The buzzards complained, but hopped to safety to wait for him to leave.

Around the remains the earth was soft and the footprints were large and deep. Murphy compared them to his. They were a full size larger than his. He followed them to where a horse had been tied and then the prints walked side by side to the horse.

He mounted the elk over the saddle and walked away.

Murphy went back for Boyle and then followed the tracks for about a mile until they disappeared at the base of a cliff.

Murphy tied Boyle to a tree and ascended the cliff three hundred feet to the top. The view was majestic with the mountains and blue sky, but he wasn't interested in the view at the moment.

Scanning below he tried to pick up any sign of John Quad that the man might have left behind.

Murphy couldn't spot a sign and came down and stood beside Boyle.

"We'll camp here the night," Murphy said as he removed the saddle from Boyle's back. "And wait."

After dark Murphy returned to the cliff, taking with him a few jerky sticks, his canteen, and a candy stick.

Slowly the moon rose and the clouds became visible in the pale light.

Murphy ate a jerky stick and took a few sips of water.

The first hint of smoke was so faint he almost didn't notice it as it reached him on a soft breeze.

He stood and scanned the dark mountains below.

The aroma grew stronger and he recognized it as meat cooking on an open fire.

From where?

How far would the scent of a fire carry in the thin mountain air?

One thousand yards?

Two?

Three thousand yards and no more than that.

Which direction?

The breeze was blowing in an easterly direction up the side of the mountain, coming from the west.

Three thousand yards to the west and below.

He wouldn't find it in the dark so he descended the cliff for the night. He covered Boyle with the two blankets and spread out his bedroll. He ate a few more sticks of jerky and then the candy stick and washed it all down with a few warming sips of his father's whiskey.

A fire was out of the question so he used the heavy bearskin coat as a blanket.

He fell asleep to the light aroma of the faraway campfire.

Five hundred feet below the ridge where he spent the night, Murphy found tracks on a path that descended another several hundred feet to a narrow ridge. He followed the ridge west with Boyle in tow behind him.

By noon or so he came upon the campsite Quad must have used the previous night. The site sat on the widest part of the path with an ascending ridge above it that was too sheer to climb.

Rocks were gathered in a circle with a spit made of sticks above the ashes. Murphy felt the ashes. They were cold. He skipped a morning fire for a cold breakfast on the run.

The path west was passable and Murphy mounted Boyle and took it at a slow walk so he could track for signs of passage.

Quad traveled the path on horseback. Murphy followed the tracks for several hundred yards until the earth became rock and he lost the trail.

"What do you think, Boyle?" Murphy asked, as he patted Boyle's neck. "Straight ahead, down, or up?"

The bullet struck directly in front of Boyle's forelimbs a full second before the report of the round sounded. Boyle reared up on his hind legs and bucked and Murphy spilled out of the saddle with his right hand holding the reins.

As Murphy hit the ground his momentum spilled him over the edge of the cliff and it was only his tight hold on the reins that saved his life.

He hung there for a moment and Quad's voice called out to him from high above.

"Whoever you are, that will teach you to follow me," Quad shouted. "If you live and follow me again, I won't miss on purpose. You've been warned. Heed it."

Murphy looked down at the sheer rocks and cliffs hundreds of feet below him. He looked up and Boyle's head was over the edge of the cliff.

"What are you waiting for, back up," Murphy said.

Boyle backed up and slowly Murphy came up and over the edge. Looking up at the sky, Murphy said, "Son of a bitch."

Murphy released the reins and slowly stood up. He rubbed Boyle's neck and gave him a few sugar cubes.

"He was up there waiting for us," Murphy said and looked up a thousand feet to an overhanging cliff.

"And as good as his advice was, we won't be following it," Murphy said and led Boyle up an incline to the next cliff.

The five-hundred-foot climb up the sheer rocks took thirty minutes. As much as Boyle didn't want to go, he followed Murphy and finally they stood on flat ground overlooking the mountains below.

"Now you stay put," Murphy said to Boyle and tied the reins to a tree.

Murphy removed the Winchester rifle from the saddle sleeve and stood close to the edge of the cliff. The view of the mountain range was breathtaking. In the distance he could see pockets of snow on peaks where trees prevented sunlight from reaching the ground.

He stood still and allowed his eyes to do the work, slowly scanning cliffs and winding paths below as they disappeared and re-appeared in various spots on the mountain.

The sun was high and bright.

Its light reflected on snow across the way.

It also reflected on movement.

Light turned to shadow and quickly back to light again when something passed through it.

Like a man on horseback.

Murphy waited patiently for twenty minutes or so, scanning below, and then he saw the shimmer of light on a path and locked onto it.

The shimmer moved along the path and Murphy cocked the lever of the Winchester and took aim. The distance was a good two thousand feet, well out of range for an accurate shot, but the tubular magazine held fifteen rounds and he fired off every one of them in quick succession.

At the crack of the first shot the shimmer stopped. Quad either dismounted or took cover in the rocks or he rode ahead out of danger.

It didn't matter.

The message that he, Murphy, was alive

and well and in pursuit was delivered loud and clear.

After the last round was fired, Murphy removed the tube from the stock and reloaded the Winchester.

As he fed .45 caliber WCF rounds into the tube, Quad's voice called out from far below.

"Who are you?" echoed Quad's voice.

"Murphy. Are you John Quad?" Murphy shouted.

"Bounty hunter?" Quad shouted.

"Lawman."

"Turn around now and go back the way you came or you'll die on this mountain," Quad shouted.

"I can't do that," Murphy shouted.

"I'll be off this mountain two days before you find the path down," Quad said. "If I see you following me on the flats I'll kill you for sure, lawman or not."

"Then that's the way it's got to be," Murphy shouted.

"You been warned, Murphy."

The magazine full, Murphy inserted the tube into the Winchester and locked it into place. He returned the rifle to the saddle and freed Boyle's reins from the tree.

"Let's find a gentle way down," Murphy said and guided Boyle.

■ ■ ■ ■

A thousand feet lower, Murphy found a spot to camp for the night on a cliff protected by higher rocks and tall pine trees. The breeze blowing up the side of the mountain took the aroma of his campfire with it, preventing it from being detected below.

He fed oats and carrots to Boyle and brushed him down while beans and bacon cooked in a fry pan. He made a pot of coffee and ate under the stars and thought about John Quad.

He said he would be off the mountain two days before Murphy reached below. Quad knew these mountains far better than he did. Why not take advantage of that knowledge and kill him?

Why leave a lawman in pursuit alive?

Quad's fight was against the railroad and government settlement program. He had no grudge against any man carrying a badge, but that only went so far. He believed Quad's warning that he would kill him if he continued pursuit. Quad wasn't going to stop his one-man war and if that meant killing Murphy if he got in the way then that was how it would be.

Quad said the *flats*.

He meant the valley south into New Mexico.

To the site of his next planned slaughter at the railroad?

Or innocent settlers?

Murphy had no way of knowing what was in Quad's enraged mind.

Only one thing was clear.

Quad wasn't going to stop and he wouldn't be taken alive.

Twenty-Four

It took a full day to find a path down the mountain to the south.

Beset with sheer cliffs, treacherous rocks, and narrow paths, Murphy guided Boyle slowly along and down until they camped less than a thousand feet above flat ground near a stream of fresh water.

Murphy filled both his canteens and prepared a large supper and a full pot of coffee. He fed Boyle oats and carrots and brushed his coat to a high shine before placing the blankets on his back.

"We have a long way to go come morning," Murphy said to Boyle. "And much longer after that."

Murphy led Boyle off the mountain two hours before sunset. He had no idea if Quad came down following the same path and he searched for signs of tracks. Several hundred yards south he picked up tracks of a lone horse weighted down, judging from the deep impressions.

Quad came down southwest off the mountain and then turned and rode south into the valley.

Murphy followed the tracks until nightfall and then made camp.

Murphy followed Quad's trail for eight hours the next day. Quad was steering clear of towns and farms, and close to sundown Murphy reached the tailing end of the Rio Grande River where it entered Colorado and ended its journey to the west.

He made camp near the river and studied his maps by the campfire. The town of Alamosa was less than a day's ride south. Unless Quad was carrying another month's worth of supplies he would have to stop and resupply.

"We're going to town tomorrow," Murphy said as he brushed Boyle beside the roaring campfire.

They came out of nowhere.

Five cowboys riding hard behind him.

Murphy kicked Boyle into a full run to keep the distance between them at rifle distance, a near impossible shot to make on horseback.

He raced Boyle to the cover of several large boulders along the foothills. He dismounted, removed the Sharps rifle from the saddle sleeve, and peered over a boulder.

At first glance they appeared to be cowboys, but on closer inspection Murphy could see they were Mexican bandits.

They crossed the border into New Mexico and went as far north as Wyoming searching for covered wagons and settlers to rob. If the wife was pretty enough they killed the husband and took her back to Mexico and sold her to a brothel. Sometimes the daughters were taken if they were old enough and pretty enough to bring a fair price.

Murphy removed a round from the bandolero and fed it into the chamber of the Sharps rifle. He waited for the five bandits to close the gap to seven hundred and fifty yards and then he aimed for the rider in the middle and pulled the trigger.

The bandit flew off his horse a full second before the other four heard the round.

Murphy quickly reloaded and shot another bandit off his horse.

The remaining three slowed their horses to a stop. They looked at the rocks where the shots seemingly came from and while they were looking Murphy shot a third dead before he hit the ground.

The two bandits left turned their horses and raced away in the opposite direction.

Murphy reloaded, aimed, and shot a fourth bandit off his horse.

He reloaded and waited for the bandit to ride to a distance of fifteen hundred yards, then took careful aim and squeezed off the shot.

The bullet struck the bandit in the back and he fell from his horse to the ground.

Murphy stood up and turned to Boyle.

"No way I could let them live," he told the horse.

Boyle snorted.

Murphy replaced the Sharps into the sleeve and dug out a few sugar cubes and fed them to Boyle.

"We best get out of here in case they have some friends lurking about," Murphy said and mounted Boyle.

Even with the delay from the bandits, Murphy was able to make the town of Alamosa by nightfall.

As western towns went, Alamosa was average in size and population. What made it important just two years after its founding was the railroad constructing a major repair and shipping facility in the town. It sat on the end of the Rio Grande River, which made transport by ship faster than freight wagons.

From a hundred yards away Murphy could hear piano and banjo music playing in a dozen saloons.

As he entered town by way of Alamosa Street, lamps on poles lit the streets and wood sidewalks and he could see the faces of what few people were out after dark.

The sheriff's office was located at the end of Main Street next to the post office. It, as well as the post office, was constructed of red brick. Light from a lantern shone through the glass window of the sheriff's office. Murphy tied Boyle to the post and stepped up to the office and opened the door.

A slim man with a mustache looked up from his desk as Murphy walked to him.

"Are you the sheriff?" Murphy asked.

"I am. Name is Quincy. Who are you?"

"Murphy," Murphy said and produced his wallet and identification and set it on the desk.

"You're a long way from home, Mr. Murphy," Quincy said. "Care for a cup of coffee while you tell me what your business is here?"

"I would."

Murphy filled a tin cup from the pot that rested atop the woodstove against the wall. He took a sip. The coffee was hot and strong.

Murphy took a chair opposite the desk.

"Are you local or county?" Murphy asked.

"Neither," Quincy said. "Railroad appointee."

"Then you know about the murders taking place in railroad camps?"

"Know about it? It's all that's talked about. What's your stake in it?"

"I'm hunting the man responsible," Murphy said. "I tracked him through the mountains and we exchanged rifle fire. He's got a two, maybe three day head start on me. He's traveling south. He might have stopped by here for supplies."

"The man responsible?" Quincy said. "For all those killings? One man?"

"His name is John Quad," Murphy said. "He's as tall as or taller than me, maybe six-foot-four or so. That alone would make him stand out. He uses a Sharps .50-90 and may need ammunition. How many stores you have in town?"

"Three dry goods and two gun shops, but all are closed until morning."

"I figured," Murphy said. "Is there a place that serves a decent steak and a hotel with a soft bed?"

"One and the same," Quincy said. "I have two deputies on patrol, mind if I join you on that steak?"

"Livery?"

"On the way to the hotel."

"That doesn't add up letting you live like that when he knew you were on his tail," Quincy said.

Murphy cut into his steak and ate a slice. He washed it down with a sip of coffee.

"He's out to punish the railroad and the government-sponsored settlers of which he was one after the war," Murphy said. "He's not after innocent people by his standards. That said, I don't think he would give me a second chance anytime soon."

"Would he have stopped for a drink? We have a dozen saloons."

"Unlikely," Murphy said. "He doesn't want to be remembered. He'd go to one store and be on his way as quickly as possible."

Quincy nodded. "Maybe one of my deputies saw him in town?"

"Possible. Let's ask them."

"If you're not in a hurry they got hot apple pie tonight for dessert."

"I've got time."

■ ■ ■ ■

Deputy Lane didn't see him, but Deputy Lundy remembered him clearly.

They met in Quincy's office and Lundy said, "He rode in close to noon two days ago. I was out front of the doc's office on Main Street and he came in riding the biggest Goddamn horse I ever seen."

"Big, how?" Quincy said. "Tall or girth?"

"Both. A quarter horse, I think."

"Did you speak to him?"

"No need," Lundy said. "He stopped at Jackson's General Store and came out with an armload of supplies. He packed them on his horse and went into Drake's Gun Shop. Then he rode out. I figured he might be a buffalo skinner by the looks of him."

"Which direction did he ride out?" Murphy said.

"South end of town."

"What time does Jackson's open?" Murphy said.

"Nine on the dot seven days a week."

"I'll say goodnight and see you at nine," Murphy said.

From the window of his room at the Alamosa Hotel, Murphy had a clear view of

Jackson's General Store.

Street lanterns on poles every thirty feet illuminated the street well enough so he could actually see goods in the windows.

Murphy sipped from a glass of his father's whiskey and smoked his pipe as he stood at the window and watched the street below.

With a two-day head start, three come tomorrow, picking up Quad's trail might prove difficult.

Unless he left some more bodies in his wake.

■ ■ ■ ■

"Yeah, I remember the big son of a bitch," Jackson said.

Jackson stood five-foot-four in boots and looked up at Murphy the way a child would their father.

"Because?" Murphy asked.

"Because he's a Goddamn giant like you," Jackson said.

"What did he buy and how did he pay?"

"He bought . . . hold on, he gave me a list," Jackson said. "I think it's still in my accounts box."

Jackson reached under the counter and brought up a cigar box. He set it down and flipped open the lid and rifled through a stack of papers.

"Here it is."

Murphy took the list.

Five pounds of beans. Five pounds of salt bacon. Five pounds flour. Five pounds coffee. Ten pounds beef jerky. One pound lard. Salt. Pepper. Six cans peaches. Six cans pears. A dozen sticks of candy. Six bars of chocolate.

"How did he pay?"

"Cash. Twelve dollars even."

Murphy looked behind the counter at the

267

shelves of ammunition.

"Ammunition?"

"No."

"Can I keep this list?"

"I don't need it."

"An artist from the Denver newspaper will be here in a few days," Murphy said. "I want you to describe him to the artist as best you can so he can draw a sketch for a poster for Sheriff Quincy here."

"I can do that," Jackson said.

"That box of .50-90 sat on the shelf more than a year," Drake said. "I figured that big fellow was after buffalo. I sold it to him for five dollars and was glad to be rid of it."

"What size box?" Murphy asked.

"Fifty rounds."

Murphy looked at Quincy. "Have the artist talk to Mr. Drake as well."

In Quincy's office, Murphy wrote out the telegram to the Denver newspaper.

"Send this today, but the poster is for railroad use only," Murphy said. "No one else sees it."

Quincy nodded. "Are you going after him alone?"

"Just as soon as I pay Mr. Jackson a visit and buy some supplies of my own."

Murphy rode Boyle south out of town where dozens of horse tracks and wagon tracks made it impossible to follow any one set.

He stayed on the southern path and slowly the tracks veered off into different directions narrowing the choices.

He stayed south and dismounted to

inspect a set of tracks that were deeper and larger than the others. The prints could have only been made by a quarter horse weighted down by a large man, his heavy weapons, supplies, and ammunition.

Murphy felt the tracks. They were dry, at least three days old.

"Well, let's see where you're going," Murphy said and mounted Boyle.

TWENTY-FIVE

Quad followed the Rio Grande south into New Mexico on the eastern side of the river. A day's ride from Santa Fe, Quad broke to the east in a direct path to the Santa Fe railroad camp.

Murphy followed the tracks, fearing the worst, hoping for the best. He arrived in the quiet, sullen camp after nightfall. Armed men were on patrol everywhere. Murphy dismounted and was met by Harold Wright, Johnson's new railroad camp police chief.

"What happened?" Murphy asked.

"Yesterday morning after the work train arrived back in camp, shots started firing from the west," Wright said. "Several men were hit before we knew what happened. The men ran for cover anywhere they could find it, some back on the train, but he just kept shooting. I didn't count, but he must have got off more than thirty rounds. Nine dead in all, six more wounded."

"Where is Mr. Johnson?" Murphy asked.

"He is one of the nine."

"Is your mess tent open?"

"Yes."

"I could use a cup of coffee."

"You men stay on patrol while I talk with Mr. Murphy," Wright told his nearby men. "And take Mr. Murphy's horse to the livery."

Murphy and Wright entered the mess tent and grabbed two cups of coffee and took seats at a vacant table.

"Mr. Johnson was a good man," Murphy said.

"Moy is overwhelmed," Wright said. "He cried like a baby when he heard the news. We'll send Mr. Johnson's body home to his family tomorrow. Moy will go with him."

"The railroad sending a new chief engineer?"

"Should be here tomorrow."

Murphy sipped from his cup.

"Why?" Wright asked. "How much blood is enough to satisfy him?"

"You can't reason with the insane," Murphy said. "How close are you to meeting the Dodge camp?"

"A week, but that was before this."

"I'll stay the night and pick up his trail in

272

the morning," Murphy said. "Can you spare a tent?"

Wright nodded. "The first man fell three seconds before we heard the shot. The son of a bitch was out there waiting for daylight. Waiting for us to get off the train."

"He won't be back this way."

"How do you know?"

"He lost a day waiting for sunup," Murphy said. "And he knows I'm on his trail. He'll want to make up time."

"Where is he going?" Wright asked.

"I don't know, but wherever that is, I'll follow."

Murphy was asleep in his tent when the sound of the flap opening woke him with a start. The Schofield .45 was in the cot with him and he cocked and aimed in one smooth motion as a lone figure entered the tent.

"Freeze or I'll drill you where you stand," Murphy said.

"It's me, Mr. Murphy. It's Moy."

Murphy lowered the Schofield, de-cocking it.

"Mr. Moy?"

"Yes, sir."

"Hold on."

Murphy sat up and struck a match and lit

the oil lantern on the small table beside the cot.

Moy's black hair glowed in the pale light.

"They said you were chasing him," Moy said. "That you were on his trail."

"Please, sit down," Murphy said.

"Is that true?"

"Yes."

Moy nodded. His eyes were bloodshot red from exhaustion and tears.

"Somebody has to stop him," he said. "Stop all this bloodshed."

"I'll fix us a drink," Murphy said. "Please, sit down."

Moy slowly sat on the folding chair beside the bed. Murphy dug the bottle of his father's whiskey out of his satchel and added some to the two water glasses beside the lantern. He gave one glass to Moy.

"I'm sorry about Mr. Johnson," Murphy said.

Moy took a small sip from his glass.

"We were still on the train in the first car with most of the men when the first shot fired," Moy said. "Mr. Johnson was the first man out to see what happened. He took the third bullet. I tried to hold him back from leaving the train, but he broke free and ran out. He died in my arms. So much blood. So much blood."

Murphy took a sip from his glass.

"Why, Mr. Murphy?" Moy nearly sobbed. "Why is he doing this?"

Murphy took another sip of his father's whiskey. "There's a great big hole in his chest where his heart used to be," he said. "And now he's trying to fill it with revenge. But no matter how hard he tries to close the hole, it stays open. That's the way it is with hate. It grips you and doesn't let go. After a while hate is all you have left and it's a powerful fuel."

"Are you talking from experience?" Moy asked.

"Mr. Moy, I'm in the mood for a good snipe hunt," Murphy said. "Will you join me, sir?"

"A snipe hunt," Moy said. "I haven't been on a snipe hunt since Mr. Johnson's youngest son was born ten years ago."

"Let me put my boots on," Murphy said.

Seated on Johnson's horse, Moy passed Murphy the nearly empty bottle of whiskey. Murphy, atop Boyle, took a sip and passed the bottle back to Moy.

"Sun's coming up," Moy said. "Will you stay for breakfast? I'll fix you Mr. Johnson's favorite."

"I could use breakfast," Murphy said.

Moy took a sip from the bottle and passed it back to Murphy.

"Where are we?" he said.

"Two, maybe three miles east of camp."

The sky began to lighten in front of them. Moy looked at the horizon.

"That hole in his chest you spoke about," Moy said. "My sense is that you have one like it. Am I wrong?"

Murphy took the bottle and took a long swallow and passed the bottle back to Moy.

"You're not wrong," Murphy said. "But the hole caused by my loss won't be filled with innocent blood spilled at my hand."

Moy nodded and drained the final ounce.

"Killing him won't, either," Moy said. "Only making peace with yourself will."

Murphy looked at the bright sliver of light on the horizon where the first hint of the sun shone through.

"Mr. Moy, I do believe I am ready for some breakfast," Mur phy said.

It wasn't that difficult to find the location where Quad waited for the work train to arrive at camp.

He made a small fire and prepared a meal.

Then he got on his stomach and waited for the train to arrive at dawn and picked off his victims as easily as swatting flies.

Murphy pulled the Sharps rifle from the sleeve and got down where Quad had and peered down the sights. He estimated the distance at fourteen hundred yards. Quad could have gone back another hundred and still made the shot, but the added distance meant a fraction of a second extra time to aim and that could have resulted in one or two less dead.

Murphy stood up and packed away the Sharps, mounted Boyle, and followed Quad's tracks south.

He rode all afternoon and made camp near Albuquerque close to the Rio Grande River. Quad's tracks made a slow, but steady progression west. He probably crossed the river at some point, but why?

To the west was nothing but desert country. An area the size of Rhode Island with nothing in it but canyons and desert. By the campfire he studied his maps. There was a flatboat river crossing ten miles to the south. If Quad crossed, that would be the place.

And if Quad crossed, he would cross.

And follow.

Twenty-Six

Quad's tracks led directly to the Rio Grande River crossing site some ten miles southwest of where Murphy had camped the previous night.

A flatboat tethered by two heavy ropes on each side of the river was manually pulled by a crew of two men across the river. The boat could hold as many as ten men and horses. Fully loaded, a one-way crossing could take fifteen minutes or more depending on the season and weather.

There was no reason to ask the boat crew if they towed Quad. His tracks led Murphy right to the boat where they abruptly ended.

Four freight wagons with eight riders and two men on horseback were already on the flatboat when Murphy arrived at the starting point. A small cabin and hitching post served as an office and living quarters for the two men who ran the boat.

"Room for one more?" Murphy said.

"Got a full load with them wagons," one of the men said. "Have a seat in the office and wait for the return. Coffee's fresh and hot on the woodstove."

Murphy tied Boyle to the post, entered the cabin and filled a mug with coffee, and then went out and sat on the steps of the cabin and lit his pipe.

Loaded down with so much weight the ride across took twice as long as the return trip, almost forty minutes total.

The two men docked the flatboat and walked to the cabin.

"We usually don't take lone passengers across," one of the men said. "Can you wait a while?"

"How much to cross?" Murphy asked.

"A dollar."

"I'll give you ten to take me across alone."

"Ten?"

"And another ten for some information."

"You a bounty hunter?"

"Lawman."

"We'll take the money in advance."

Murphy dug out his wallet and counted out twenty dollars and handed it to one of the men.

"I'm after a man who crossed on your towboat two days ago," Murphy said.

"Thirty men have crossed since then."

"He's six-four or taller, carried a Buffalo gun, and rides a massive horse," Murphy said. "How many like that?"

Murphy watched the opposite shore of the Rio Grande come closer as the two men pulled on the thick tow ropes. The ride took just ten or twelve minutes. Once docked, Murphy led Boyle onto land.

The two men followed Murphy and stood by his side.

"He went due south," one of the men said.

"You're sure?" Murphy said.

"I'm sure. He didn't say two words the whole time and everyone else rode west away from the desert except him."

"Thanks," Murphy said and mounted Boyle.

Murphy followed Quad's trail for several miles south until Quad made a turn southwest following the river and then Murphy broke for a late lunch and to give Boyle a breather. It was hot, although not as hot as it would be in July or August when the temperature in the desert canyons would scorch a man exposed to the sun, dry him out like leather, and leave him for buzzard food.

Murphy ate some jerky and a can of

peaches, drinking every drop of syrup in the can. He gave Boyle three carrot sticks from the batch of a dozen he had bought at the general store and some sugar cubes, then brushed the salt from his coat and allowed him to cool down.

The Rio Grande flowed all the way to Texas into Mexico; would Quad follow it the entire way? Was his plan to hide out in Mexico, maybe even take up residence there?

The only way to know for sure was to stay in pursuit.

Murphy mounted Boyle and rode to sundown, following Quad's trail. They were on the fringe of entering the desert and if Quad went south, then Murphy went south.

Once the sun set, the temperature dropped twenty degrees or more and Murphy made a fire and cooked a hot meal. He fed Boyle oats and a few sticks of carrots and then draped the thin blanket around his back.

Exhausted, Murphy fell into a deep sleep and didn't stir until the sun in his eyes woke him.

Around noon the following day, Murphy lost Quad's trail. He dismounted and checked for signs, walked back to the last point before the trail vanished, and scanned the area.

Murphy looked across the Rio Grande. If a man were to cross it, this would be the place. Three hundred feet across and shallower than at the flatboat crossing, a man on horseback could make it if the horse were steady enough.

"He crossed the river," Murphy said to Boyle. "The son of a bitch crossed the river. Why?"

Murphy mounted Boyle and rubbed his neck.

"It's not too deep here, boy," he said. "You can swim it. It's the first step down that's the scary one."

As Murphy brought Boyle to the embankment of the river, he didn't hear the bullet that grazed his forehead and knocked him unconscious to the ground.

The sun was low in the sky when Murphy opened his eyes. Dried blood was in his mouth. He coughed and spit and sat up. Immediately overwhelmed by nausea, he rolled over and vomited a vile liquid.

When his stomach was empty, he sat up and dizziness struck and he flopped onto his back to wait for it to pass.

When his eyes came into focus and his stomach settled, he sat up. Boyle was gone.

A few feet away his saddlebags and two canteens, bedroll, and Winchester rifle sat undisturbed on the ground.

Quad wrote two words in the dirt.

1700 yards.

Bracing his arms against the ground, Murphy managed to get to his feet.

He looked at the tracks that went west. Quad had Boyle in tow. He purposely led him on a wild goose chase, double backed, and got the jump on him.

The note in the dirt was to let him know his intention was not to kill him. The maximum effective killing range of the .50-90 was fifteen hundred yards. After that a shot would have to hit you directly in the throat to kill you. At seventeen hundred yards the bullet that struck him on the left temple had the force of a whiskey bottle swung powerfully at close range. Enough to knock you cold but leave you alive.

Murphy checked the saddlebags. Quad left him his supplies, bedroll, and ammunition for the Winchester and Schofield pistol. He had taken the ammunition for the Sharps, including the bandoliers.

He felt the left side of his face. It was caked with dried blood. He walked down the embankment of the river and got on his belly and plunged his face into the water.

The cold water stung his sunburned skin, but washed the blood away and when he rolled over he felt some strength return to his body.

There was nothing to do now except build a fire, eat something for strength, and try to rest for tomorrow.

Murphy sat with his back against the saddle, facing the fire, and ate beans, bacon, and a can of peaches. He made coffee and found the last bottle of his father's whiskey intact in the saddlebags. He added a splash to his cup.

Then he poured a bit of whiskey into his hand and dabbed it on the cut on his forehead. The whiskey burned on his skin and in his throat as he sipped from the cup.

He pulled out the tobacco pouch and filled his pipe and smoked while he drank his coffee.

He thought about his options.

He could walk the fifteen plus miles back to the flatboat ferry and try to buy a horse. In his condition and carrying forty plus pounds of saddlebags it would take him two full days to reach the boat.

Quad would be long gone and any chance of picking up his trail would be lost until he killed again.

He could follow Quad's tracks on foot and

hope that Quad camped out for a few days believing he would never follow him west into the desert.

Neither option was desirable.

Walking back to the flatboat was probably more survivable.

But that gave Quad the opportunity to kill again or escape into hiding.

Then there was Boyle. He spent years training that horse and he was not about to lose him without a fight.

He took a final sip from his cup and spread out the bedroll.

Sleep was almost immediate.

But rest was not.

Because every day spent fighting the war was better than every day behind a plow. Because the guilt of deserting your family and because the prospect of war was more exciting and fulfilling than spending your life behind the ass end of a mule.

Because you want your soul back and the only way to get that is through self-forgiveness and how do you absolve your sins when you know in your heart that you are guilty of them?

Murphy opened his eyes to the rising sun.

Sally was right.

It was time to bury the dead and start living.

If he survived the desert, he would go to Saint Louis and tell her that very thing.

Murphy cooked the rest of the bacon for breakfast. He dumped the flour and kept just the beans, jerked beef, coffee, and canned fruit. He took the canteens to the river and filled both to the top.

He removed the last bottle of his father's whiskey from the saddlebags and dumped the entire contents on the ground. The scorching sun and whiskey are a bad combination, especially if you're on foot with limited water.

He took the bottle to the river and rinsed out any residue of whiskey and then filled it with fresh water, replaced the cork, and tucked it away in the saddlebags.

Saddlebags packed, Murphy lifted them and draped them around his neck like a forty pound scarf, picked up the Winchester rifle, and followed Quad's tracks west.

Twenty-Seven

The noon sun was scorching hot and Murphy set down the saddlebags and took refuge in the shade of a lone desert tree. The back of his neck ached from carrying the forty-pound bags and as thirsty as he was he didn't drink. Water would just make him sweat even more. It was best to wait until dark to take water. Instead he poured a little on his neckerchief and wiped his face and the back of his neck.

Rested, he stood up, loaded on the saddlebags, and plodded on for several more hours, following Quad's tracks. Boyle was still in tow, riding slightly behind Quad's horse.

Late in the day, Murphy felt the skin on his face start to bubble from the scorching hot sun.

He stopped to rest again and cooled down his skin with a wet neckerchief.

With two hours to sundown, Murphy

picked himself up and continued walking. The forty-pound saddlebags on his neck felt like an iron anvil. His boots, soaked with sweat, felt like bricks.

Yet he carried on and didn't stop until dark. He had no idea how far he traveled but ten or twelve miles seemed about right.

He sat and took several long swallows from a canteen. Then he gathered up sticks, twigs, brush, and anything else that would burn and made a fire. He poured a few ounces of water into the fry pan, filled it with beans, and set it directly onto the fire.

He ate a stick of jerky while the beans boiled.

He didn't make coffee. He left the pot back at the Rio Grande because it weighed several pounds and he didn't need the extra weight to carry and he couldn't spare the water to brew a pot anyway.

He ate the beans with a spoon and afterward allowed himself to take two more sips of water.

Then he spread out the bedroll and fell asleep near the fire.

The cold desert air woke him up several hours later. A furnace during the day, an icebox at night. He quickly gathered up some brush and sticks, made another fire, and crawled back inside the bedroll.

■ ■ ■ ■

By noon the next day, Murphy was in the thick of it. Desert and tall canyons and dry as a bone. He wasn't sure if he was in New Mexico or Arizona, but did that matter? The signs left by Quad and two horses were easy enough to follow and as long as he could still walk he would stay in pursuit.

As he stopped to rest he examined the tall canyon walls around him. They were as beautiful as they were deadly. The same could be said for the desert. He wanted water, but resisted the urge to drink and instead wiped his face with a wet neckerchief.

A reflection glinting atop a canyon wall caught his eye, but when he turned to look up, it was gone.

He shielded his eyes with his hands and searched for the source of the glint, but whatever the cause of it escaped him.

He pulled himself to his feet, lifted saddlebags and Winchester, and followed Quad's trail through a box canyon.

The tall canyon walls provided some much needed shade, a welcome relief to the hot sun. He walked a mile before he caught a fleeting glimpse of a reflection of light from the canyon high up on his left.

It wasn't his imagination. The reflection was real and could only be caused by something or someone up there following him.

Bandits?

They would have struck, robbed him, and left him for dead by now.

Quad?

Possibly?

He could be up there watching him and enjoying seeing him slowly die from heat and exhaustion.

Why waste a bullet when the desert will do the job for you?

Murphy walked another mile and decided to take a short rest. He picked out a rock in the shade of the canyon wall to sit on, removed the saddlebags from around his shoulders, and took a seat.

His neck and back ached; his legs were weak at the knees. He was dehydrated and needed water. There were a few hours left before dark, but he needed a sip of water to continue, so he opened one canteen and took a thirsty swallow.

He poured a little water on his hand and dabbed his face.

Then he lifted his gear and pressed on through the canyon. Another mile and his head started to ache where Quad's bullet grazed him. He needed to stop and rest and save his strength.

The sun was brutal.

He sat on a rock for few minutes, took a small sip of water, and wet his face again. When he stood and lifted his gear, he felt dizzy and weak. Just a few hours to sundown and the air would turn cool and he could rest for the night.

He walked.

For how long or far he didn't know.

The back of his neck blistered.

He slowly became aware that he was no longer carrying his gear and Winchester. He turned and saw that he dropped them a hundred feet or so behind him. He slowly walked back to the gear, lifted the bags and Winchester, and moved forward again.

A glint of light atop the canyon walls reflected in his face and Murphy glanced up, but again its source escaped him.

"Well . . . ," Murphy gasped. "I'm here. Come on if you're coming."

He walked another hundred yards through the canyon and the gear and Winchester fell from his arms. The sun and the heat took everything he had and there was nothing left.

He stood there in the sun, baking, and

then he saw the glint of light again and when he looked up, right before he passed out, Murphy saw the face of an Apache Indian looking down on him.

Sweat ran down his forehead and stung his eyes.

At the same time his teeth chattered from freezing cold.

And naked and smelling of sweet bath oils, his wife, Katherine, came to him in bed the night before he left her to fight in a war he had no stake in. She was on top and as she put her head back he looked into the face of Sally Orr, who smiled sweetly at him.

Singing in the background.

Someone was singing.

An Apache death chant.

For him?

Freezing cold.

On a raid of a small camp of Rebel soldiers, they chose to fight to the last man rather than surrender.

The last man was a fifteen-year-old boy from Mississippi.

Why didn't that stupid kid surrender?

Why did you make me kill you?

Because you believed in your cause.

And you died for it.

Clouds, dark and angry, rolled by and sud-

denly they took the shape of a man, an Apache, and the Apache was digging a grave.

For him?

The clouds started to rain, only the rain wasn't water but tears.

And he looked into the face of John Quad and saw himself.

Two different men haunted by their past and driven by guilt, shame, and revenge.

Murphy opened his eyes and looked up at a bright, blue sky. He was under a green, wool blanket. A rolled blanket under his head served as a pillow. To his right a fire crackled. To his left a dozen horses grazed lazily on green grass.

Directly in front of him a dozen Apache warriors sat around a much larger campfire and ate meat from a small deer that roasted on a spit.

Murphy tried to sit up under the blanket and dizziness struck and he moaned as he fell back.

An Apache stood up from the group and walked to Murphy.

He was a tall, well put together fellow with a rugged, handsome face well-worn by the Arizona sun. He spoke in a rich, baritone voice and in English.

"I am Ten Moons, chief of my people," he said.

"You speak English very well," Murphy said.

"And French and Spanish," Ten Moons said.

"That was you on the cliff?"

"Yes."

"You saved my life?"

"Yes."

"Why?"

Ten Moons shrugged. "Why not?"

Murphy felt the bandage on his forehead. "Who did this?"

"Our medicine man is a doctor educated back east," Ten Moons said. "He cares for all on the reservation and sometimes helps out at the Army post in Winston. Since we couldn't bring you to him I brought him to you."

"How long was I out?"

"Three days. Are you hungry?"

"What's on the spit?"

"Venison."

"I'm starved. Can you help me up?"

Ten Moons gave Murphy a hand and once on his feet, although weak in the knees, he was able to walk to the circle of Apache braves.

"Sit. Eat," Ten Moons said.

Murphy lowered himself into a cross-legged position between the braves. "Do they all speak English?"

"I taught them the language," Ten Moons said. "The way my father's father taught him and he taught me, but they will not speak unless I give them permission."

Murphy understood. Before eighteen hundred, when the west belonged to France and Spain those countries brought with them their culture and language. Indian tribes, if they wanted to exist and trade with the French and Spanish had to learn the languages. Even after the Louisiana Purchase there was still a strong French and Spanish influence in the states and territories and it was not unusual to speak three or more languages, white man and Indian.

Ten Moons sat beside Murphy.

"Eat," Ten Moons said.

A brave used his knife to slice off a hunk of steak and handed it to Murphy.

"Obliged," Murphy said.

With his strength returning, Murphy and Ten Moons walked beside the sheer cliff of a canyon wall.

"Very pretty country," Murphy said.

"Much like the diamondback," Ten Moons

said. "It draws you near with its beauty and when you are close, it shows you how deadly it can be."

Murphy touched his bandage. "And the sun."

"I went through your papers," Ten Moons said. "You are a government man named Murphy."

"Yes."

"You are a lawman?"

"Of sorts."

"You are after the big man with two horses?"

Murphy nodded. "One of them is mine. He double backed on me by the Rio Grande River and got the jump on me from behind. He took my horse, but left me supplies and water."

"Why didn't he kill you?"

"I don't know," Murphy said. "Maybe because I'm not who he's after."

"Is he the railroad killer of men?"

"Yes."

"I have heard the stories," Ten Moons said. "His heart is twisted from hate."

"He blames the railroad and the government settler program for the death of his wife and baby and for spending twelve years in prison," Murphy said. "I believe him to be right about that, but not how he's seeking justice."

"Giving pain for pain doesn't bring back the dead or change the past," Ten Moons said. "It only consumes us with hate and twists our heart."

Murphy nodded. "How did you come to be following me?"

"We capture wild horses from the canyons and sell them to the Army," Ten Moons said. "It is an arrangement we've had since seventy-four. We were checking for horses when I spotted the big man with two horses riding through. Two days later I saw you on foot and watched you until you collapsed. I was curious how far you could walk."

"Where was he headed, do you know?"

"Into the forest of rock trees."

"The Petrified Forest?"

"Yes."

"Can I get the use of a horse and saddle?" Murphy asked. "I promise to return them or give something of equal value."

Ten Moons nodded.

"Appreciate it."

"You will leave in the morning after a night's rest."

"Yes."

"Our medicine man will be here tonight to check your bandage."

"Do you have a hospital on the reservation?"

"A small one. Beds for six."

"Do you have a pipe?"

"Yes."

"Let's go back to the fire and smoke."

Two Bears, named because by age ten he had shot and killed two grizzly bears with a Hawken .50 caliber rifle, took the name Morgan Lambert after his teachers Mr. Morgan, and Mr. Lambert, in school in Boston when he was fourteen years old.

A dozen years earlier, after the treaty with the government and Christian brothers and teachers came to the newly settled reservation, he learned so quickly that the brothers sponsored him to his education.

Now twenty-six years old, Morgan lived and worked as a doctor on the reservation and the Army post in Winston as needed.

Murphy thought Morgan a handsome man in his black suit with his dark ponytail tucked down his back. He carried a doctor's black medical bag by the campfire and removed the bandage from Murphy's forehead.

"That's coming along fine," Morgan said. "I'm going to give you some clean wraps and a bottle of alcohol. When you change the wraps, pour some alcohol on it and allow it to soak into the skin."

"How much for the house call?" Murphy asked.

"I draw a government salary," Morgan said.

"I understand you have a small hospital on the reservation?" Murphy said.

"Too small."

Murphy opened his saddlebags and dug to the bottom and pulled up the false flap where the expense money was hidden in a thick envelope. He removed five thousand dollars and handed it to Morgan.

"Make it bigger," Murphy said.

Morgan looked at the inch-thick stack of bills. "This is a lot of money."

"You need a lot of hospital," Murphy said.

Morgan looked at Ten Moons, and the chief nodded.

"I do at that," Morgan said.

"Will you stay the night?" Murphy asked.

Morgan nodded.

"Good. Then you can check my head before I leave in the morning."

Ten Moons held the reins to a large male pinto saddled with an Army regulation saddle and bridle.

"I hope you don't mind a spotted horse,"

Ten Moons said. "He can run all day and doesn't spook easily."

"He's fine, Ten Moons," Murphy said. "Thank you."

Ten Moons extended his right hand to Murphy and they shook firmly.

"If I live through this, I'll stop and visit sometime," Murphy said.

Twenty-Eight

After a day's ride west through the canyon pass, Quad's trail led to the Petrified Forest in northern Arizona.

Murphy made camp a few miles from the forest just before dark. He tended to the pinto first, then made a fire and tended to his bandage. The lump was nearly gone and the scab had dried out.

He brushed the pinto and gave him oats and a few sugar cubes. Ten Moons was correct when he said the horse could run all day and didn't spook. Murphy had the feeling the pinto was meant for an Army officer.

After eating a quick supper, Murphy checked his maps by the campfire. Quad was traveling southwest at this point.

To where?

To the south was Winslow.

To the west was Flagstaff.

He dug out the list of railroad construction sites given to him by Bradley and read the locations. A new line was being developed by the Santa Fe for the purposes of carrying freight from Flagstaff west to Kingman, and another from Flagstaff south to Scottsdale.

Flagstaff was likely the first target.

To reach Flagstaff, Murphy would have to cross fifty thousand square acres of the desert called the Petrified Forest.

The pinto was up for the three-day, thirty-mile journey.

His concussion was better and so was he.

They would leave at first light before the sun rose and scorched the earth.

The Petrified Forest, so called for its many samples of petrified fossils and trees, was as beautiful to look at in morning sun as it was deadly. Especially the badlands area, easily seen by the reddish clay dirt and blue coral.

By ten in the morning, Murphy estimated the temperature to be around ninety degrees or higher.

The pinto more than held his own in the heat.

Surrounded by rocks, hills, and small mountains, Murphy guided the pinto on flat land as much as possible. He kept his eyes on the darkening clouds in the distance. They were growing and moving east quickly.

"A flash storm is headed our way," Murphy told the pinto. "Best look for some cover."

Shortly before the storm hit, Murphy spotted an excavation cave on the side of a tall hill and he rode the pinto to it and dismounted. The cave was large enough for the pinto to fit into.

Murphy gathered up some sage and dry twigs and built a fire inside the cave and then led the pinto inside.

A few minutes later, the storm arrived and dumped massive amounts of rain in a very short time.

Murphy opened both canteens and the whiskey bottle and set them outside on a tall rock to catch as much rain as possible.

The pinto seemed unfazed by the storm, or the river that flowed past the cave. As Murphy rubbed his neck, he noticed the drawings on the walls of the cave.

Warriors engaged in combat with decorative shields. Others in some kind of ceremonial dance. Depictions of animals and sea life. Some kind of god.

The drawings had been there a thousand or more years and were the reason the site had been excavated.

In less than twenty minutes, the storm had passed. Outside the cave, the river was a trickle of a stream.

Murphy led the pinto outside the cave and gathered up canteens and bottle.

Across the forest, steam rose up from the ground as water evaporated.

Murphy mounted the pinto and they rode until close to sunset.

He gathered as much brush and wood as possible and built a large campfire. Scorching hot during the day, after dark the temperature in the forest dropped to forty degrees or less.

As he ate a quick supper, Murphy figured another day's ride out of the forest and maybe he could pick up Quad's trail to Flagstaff. Hopefully before Quad killed again.

The change of scenery told Murphy they had traveled through the Petrified Forest shortly past noon.

Not that the landscape was a Garden of Eden, but tall cactus trees, flowers, and sage were prevalent throughout.

After another day's ride, mountains loomed large in the background. Flat ground gave way to rolling hills with green grass and he stopped to camp beside a small stream so the pinto could eat and drink his fill.

By the campfire, Murphy checked his maps.

He was a day and a half from the site of the Flagstaff connector railroad south to Prescott.

Murphy was betting that short on supplies, Quad would ride into Flagstaff. The question was, would Quad go to Flagstaff before or after he shot up the railroad camp?

From a distance, Murphy could see the black smoke of a train locomotive on the horizon. He rode until he was a half mile from the source and then dismounted the pinto on a tall hill.

With the binoculars, Murphy watched as six men dug graves a hundred feet from the new track while workers pounded rails.

His question of what Quad would do next was answered.

Flagstaff was a large town, brimming with wealth and activity. Situated just west of the largest ponderosa pine forest in the country, the trees brought industry, prosperity, and the railroad to the quickly growing town.

Riding into a crowded Main Street, Murphy stopped in front of the sheriff's office, a red brick building that stood alone at the end of the street.

Justin Perry had been sheriff of Flagstaff going on three years. He was a tough lawman from Arkansas, with a reputation for fairness when earned and discipline when needed, and was exactly the kind of sheriff Flagstaff needed.

He employed three deputies, one of whom was in the office with him when Murphy entered.

Perry looked up from his desk at Murphy as he walked toward him. Drinking coffee beside the desk, Deputy Kemp lowered his right hand to touch his Colt Peacemaker.

"That's not necessary, Deputy," Murphy said.

"I'm Sheriff James Perry, who are you?" Perry asked.

Murphy dug his wallet out of his pocket and set it on the desk. "Name is Murphy."

Perry read the identification and looked at Murphy. "Long ways from Washington, Mr. Murphy," he said. "What brings you to Flagstaff?"

"The five dead men being buried out at the railroad extension," Murphy said.

"We heard," Perry said. "You're here about that?"

"I've been sent from Washington to find a

man named Quad and stop him from murdering railroad workers and settlers," Murphy said. "You must know about that by now."

"We're kind of removed here in Flagstaff," Perry said. "News can sometimes get here slow, but yes, we do know about it."

"John Quad blames the railroad for the death of his family and for spending twelve years in federal prison," Murphy said.

"And he killed those five men and you think he's here in town?" Perry asked.

"Yes."

"Why would he murder five men in cold blood and then ride into town like he was going to a Sunday school picnic?" Perry asked.

"I've been on his trail for weeks," Murphy said. "He needs supplies, and like you said, you're kind of removed here. Nobody knows what he looks like around here, so he could ride in, get what he needs and ride out, and who would know?"

"What does he look like?"

"As tall, or taller than me," Murphy said. "Rides a large horse. Carries a Sharps rifle and Schofield pistol."

"Jim?" Kemp said.

"What?"

"I know where that man is."

Murphy spun around to Kemp. "Where?"

"Hotel across the street. I saw him yesterday buying supplies at the general store and then he checked into the hotel across the street."

Murphy turned and took a step toward the door.

"What do you think you're doing?" Perry said.

"Going after him."

"No, you're not," Perry said. "That's our job."

"Sheriff, he's not to be taken lightly."

"Look, Mr. Murphy, we're just a small sheriff's department, but we're expected to do our job. My deputy and I will go over to the hotel and you're welcome to go with us, but this is my town and you'll obey the law."

"I never said I wouldn't," Murphy said.

"Let's go then," Perry said.

"Checked out at dawn," the clerk at the hotel desk said.

"Did he say anything?" Perry asked.

"No, Sheriff. Just paid his bill and left. Had a bunch of supplies in his room he picked up at the general store last night. I saw him load them onto his horse before he rode out."

"One horse or two?" Murphy asked.

"One."

Murphy found Boyle in the livery stable saddled and ready to go. Quad no longer had use for him and probably decided he could make better time without a second horse in tow.

"That's my horse," Murphy told the stable owner. "The man who left him here stole him from me. My name is carved under the saddle. Take a look."

"What is your name?" the stable manager said.

Murphy dug out his wallet as the stable manager removed the saddle and saw the name *Murphy* carved into the leather.

"I have a pinto outside," Murphy said. "You can keep him in its place. He's a fine, gentle horse."

"One thing," the stable manager said. "Your horse has seen some hard riding. He needs four new shoes. Best take him to the blacksmith if you plan riding more than a mile or two."

Murphy took Boyle to the blacksmith for new shoes and used the time to shop for supplies at the general store while Boyle was being fitted. He stopped at the sheriff's office after buying goods.

"My authority ends a hundred feet from

the town line or I'd go with you a ways," Perry said.

"No need," Murphy said. "Just letting you know I'll be riding out as soon as my horse is fitted with new shoes."

"Good luck to you," Perry said.

Murphy nodded and left the office.

Quad had more than a three-hour head start by the time he rode north out of town.

Twenty-Nine

Murphy rode due north and picked up Quad's trail easily enough. Quad rode his massive horse at a blistering pace, counting on distance and nightfall to lose himself in open country.

By dark, Murphy made camp and tended to Boyle first.

As he brushed Boyle's back and side, Murphy said, "It looks like that long vacation I promised you will have to wait awhile longer, I'm afraid."

Boyle responded to Murphy's voice and turned his head.

"It can't be helped," Murphy said. "And all things considered, I'd rather be in Saint Louis."

Quad's trail led to a tributary of the Colorado River, a small river flowing southwest into Arizona.

On the other side of the tributary was the

Painted Desert and Quad's trail led directly into it.

Murphy camped early by the tributary stream to give Boyle extra rest and water for the ride into the desert.

By the campfire Murphy studied his map.

Sixty miles of desert to cross into Utah, if that's where Quad was headed, and his tracks indicated so.

Murphy looked at Boyle.

"I know what you're thinking," he said. "But it can't be helped."

If it weren't for the scorching dry heat, the Painted Desert would be a treat for the eyes. Red clay, mixed with teals and blues on rocks, hills, and flat ground, made it seem like you were riding into a painting.

Then you felt the sun on your neck and the reality of where you were brought you back down to earth.

An hour into the desert, Murphy picked up Quad's trail. He was riding northwest, a route that led to Bryce Canyon in Utah.

"As good a place as any to lose yourself," Murphy said to Boyle.

The third day crossing the desert, Murphy spotted a black dot on the horizon and dismounted Boyle and dug out the binoculars.

The dot was Quad.

He was holding the Sharps rifle with a white neckerchief tied to it and standing beside a campfire.

"Looks like he wants a parlay," Murphy told Boyle.

He removed the Sharps rifle from the saddle sleeve and tied his white neckerchief to the muzzle and slung one canteen over

313

his right shoulder.

"Don't make me have to call you," Murphy told Boyle and started walking.

Walking slowly, but steadily across the sand, it took twenty minutes for Murphy to travel the two-thousand-yard distance to Quad.

When ten feet separated them, they stood with Sharps on shoulders and sized one another up like enemies on the battlefield.

Quad was several inches taller than Murphy, and a good twenty pounds heavier. Surprisingly, Quad was clean-shaven as if he'd just visited a barber. His dark eyes were filled with pain and something else Murphy couldn't identify.

"I'm Murphy, are you Quad?" Murphy asked.

"You're one stubborn son of a bitch, I'll give you that," Quad said. "I gave you five-to-one odds of making it through the desert on foot."

"I thought it right considerate that you didn't outright kill me," Murphy said.

"You earned your respect. I didn't think any one man could keep pace with me. Besides, I figured the desert would do that. Want some coffee? I just made it."

"Sure."

Quad reached for the pot and filled a tin

cup and gave it to Murphy, and then filled a second one for him.

Murphy sipped. "You make good coffee."

"So let's get down to it," Quad said. "Are you law or bounty?"

"Law," Murphy said.

"They send you to stop me?"

"You're killing innocent people," Murphy said. "Did you think they would let you get away with that?"

"Innocent people?" Quad said. "Innocent of what?"

"I know what happened to you," Murphy said. "But the people you're killing had nothing to do with that."

"I came back from the war and took my family west because the government offered good land cheap for those willing to work hard," Quad said. "I built a home, started a family, and then the railroad came and told us the land I bought and sweated over was no longer mine. They set fire to my cabin. My wife and baby died and I was sent to prison for twelve years. Who pays for that, Murphy? Who answers for my wife and child and twelve years spent in a stinking federal prison?"

"I don't know," Murphy said. "But it isn't the people you're taking it out on."

"What would you know about it, lawman?"

"You think you're the only one that lost family?" Murphy said. "When I was away fighting the war some deserters invaded my home, raped my wife, and burned the house down with her and my child in it. Six men and I spent years hunting them down and I killed them all, but they were guilty. The men and families you're killing are not."

"I was with Sherman," Quad said. "You?"

"Grant."

Quad stared at Murphy for several long seconds. "You're that Murphy? Colonel Murphy?"

"That was a long time ago," Murphy said.

"That's why they sent you for me, isn't it?" Quad asked. "Because we both know what it's like to have everything you care about ripped away like wings off a fly."

"They sent me because I knew how to find you," Murphy said. "That's why they sent me."

Murphy sipped coffee and stared at Quad. The something he couldn't identify in Quad's eyes earlier suddenly became clear. It was absolute pure hatred for the human race.

"So what now?" Murphy asked. "Now that I've found you."

Quad stared at Murphy. Then he sipped coffee and said, "Before when I left you in the desert I wondered who you were and what kind of a man you were. Now I know. Now that we have spoken face-to-face and shared a cup of coffee, it would bother me to have to kill you. But understand this, once this parlay is over and if you continue to pursue me, I won't hesitate for one second to kill you."

Murphy nodded. "We have shared coffee and words, that is true, and now that I have looked into your eyes it would bother me as well to kill you, but understand that what you are doing is wrong and you must be stopped. Once this parlay is over I will continue to hunt you and I also won't hesitate for one second to kill you."

"My horse is two thousand yards to the north," Quad said. "The parlay ends when we are mounted."

"Then that's the way it is," Murphy said. "Thank you for a fine cup of coffee."

"You're welcome."

Murphy fed Boyle a few sugar cubes as he stroked his long, muscular neck.

"He's gone into the canyons, boy," Murphy said. "And I'm afraid we'll be going after him. He'll look for a place to set a trap for us, so we'll have to be extra careful and not let that happen."

Boyle snorted and turned his head to look at Murphy.

"I know what you're thinking, that we are a very stupid pair," Murphy said.

He took the reins and mounted Boyle.

"It's the only way to save my soul," he said.

THIRTY

Bryce Canyon loomed large and imposing as Murphy rode north into a pass. Colorful, with thousands of jutting rock formations that more resembled an ancient amphitheatre than an actual canyon, there were a thousand places to hide and spring a trap.

A half mile into the canyon, Murphy decided to make camp early. He fed and brushed Boyle and then built a fire from brush and dry twigs and wood he gathered from the canyon floor.

He ate and smoked, and waited for the moon to rise. When it did, he extinguished the fire and allowed his eyes time to adjust to the darkness.

The moon was a day from being full and bright enough to illuminate the colors of the rocks and canyon walls, bright enough to cast shadows.

He studied the floors, walls, rocks, and trails ahead and above. With his night vision at one hundred percent, he could easily traverse even a sheer cliff, or ride Boyle along a path.

In the distance, a wolf howled and was answered by another wolf.

Boyle snorted and nervously stomped his right, front leg. Murphy rubbed his neck and said, "They won't bother us, boy. Don't fret about it. Let's get some sleep."

Murphy hobbled Boyle with leather strips around his legs, covered him with the heavy wool blanket, and softly rubbed his neck.

Murphy spread his bedroll on the ground and used his saddlebags as a pillow and stared up at the million stars overhead and the brilliant moon lighting the canyon floor.

As he closed his eyes, he thought, what a perfect place to die.

THIRTY-ONE

Surrounded by walls of red and floors a golden copper, Murphy rode through the canyon, following Quad's trail until the trail ended.

Murphy dismounted.

He scanned the surrounding mountains and rocks and realized he was standing in the bottom of a giant natural amphitheatre almost too beautiful to describe in words.

"You wait here for a bit," Murphy told Boyle.

Taking the Winchester rifle, Murphy looked for signs on the embankment to his left, climbing to the top without noticing any sign that a man and horse recently passed through.

He came down and tried the wall on his left and reached the summit with the same results.

Looking at the magnificent view of summits and peaks glowing in the afternoon sun, Murphy said aloud, "What are you up to, John? Where are you?"

Murphy came down and stood beside Boyle and gently rubbed his neck.

The sun moved slowly across the sky and his shadow was behind him and Murphy turned around and then looked up at the wall behind him to the right.

"Why not?" he said and gave Boyle a pat on the neck.

Backtracking on foot, Murphy walked several hundred feet and spotted a small pile of rocks he missed earlier. They came from the summit above. He knelt down and picked up a few pebbles.

Looking up, Murphy said, "Okay, John."

Murphy returned to Boyle and gave him a good brushing and grain and a few sugar cubes, then hobbled him as the sun started to set.

All around him the colors of the peaks and summits glowed as the sunlight glistened off them.

"Ever see such a sight, boy?" Murphy asked Boyle.

He gathered brush and sticks and built a fire and smoked his pipe while he sat in front of it.

He ate a few jerky sticks and washed them down with sips of water.

The sun set and the canyon walls were blanketed in darkness.

Murphy added some brush and a few sticks to the fire.

The full moon slowly came up and a few shadows appeared on the walls and ground.

Murphy spread his bedroll on the ground and stuffed it with his saddlebags.

He dug up some clay and placed it in his fry pan and added some water. He used a stick to stir it up and create a thick mud paste. He smeared the mud paste of the metal plate and lever of the Winchester until it was as dark as the wood stock and blued barrel.

He waited for the moon to rise a bit more and his night vision to reach one hundred percent.

Then he climbed the wall of the canyon to his right to the summit and waited in the shadows.

Below, the campfire slowly faded and died out.

Murphy avoided looking at the bright moon to keep his night vision sharp. He kept an eye on Boyle. The horse was still and calm, almost asleep.

And then Boyle snorted softly and Murphy could see the horse nervously wiggle his ears a bit.

Murphy watched the floor of the canyons.

Quad's elongated shadow preceded him. He moved slowly, quietly, the way he was trained to do as an Army sniper.

Twenty feet from the bedroll, Quad went down to his hands and knees and silently crawled toward it.

The Sharps rifle was looped around Quad's back with a sling. A long hunting knife was clenched between his teeth.

When he reached the bedroll, Quad took the knife from his teeth into his left hand, flung the bedroll open, and stabbed down at the saddlebags.

Instantly recognizing the trap, Quad jumped to his feet.

"I'm here, Quad," Murphy said from the shadows on the summit.

Quad pulled the Sharps rifle from the sling, aimed, and fired at Murphy's voice.

The shot went wide. Quad ran into the shadows, Murphy slid down the canyon a hundred feet to the ground.

Quad was gone.

The canyon was silent.

Murphy followed Quad down the dark canyon pass.

"Let me take you in, John," Murphy said. "I promise you won't do another day in prison. Just a hospital for men like you with problems."

Murphy stood still and listened.

Pebbles and dirt rolled down the canyon to his right. Murphy looked up at the brightly lit canyon wall. Holding the Winchester in both arms, he climbed to the summit and stood motionless in the shadows.

A hundred feet in front of him, Quad moved from shadow to light and back into shadow again.

Murphy hugged the shadows as he walked along the summit toward Quad.

As he neared the area where he had spotted Quad's shadow, Quad suddenly leapt from one summit top to another and vanished into darkness.

Quad was trying to draw him in for a shot with the Sharps. His Schofield pistol was useless in the dark past twenty feet. Since the Sharps only held one round at a time, Quad needed to make sure the shot hit the mark, because in the few seconds it took to eject, reload, cock, and fire, Murphy could get off five or six shots with the Winchester.

Murphy ducked behind a rock in darkness.

"John Quad, listen to me now," he said. "We don't have to do this. I give you my word they'll send you to a hospital for treatment."

Murphy heard a noise, looked, and saw Quad jump to another summit.

Murphy stood, went to the edge, and jumped to the next summit top. As he landed, he saw Quad in the moonlight, the Sharps aimed at him.

Murphy threw himself to the ground as Quad fired.

The bullet whizzed over Murphy's head and the missed shot echoed loudly in the surrounding canyons.

Murphy rolled over and aimed the Winchester at the spot where Quad had been, but no longer was, and fired six rounds.

Murphy quickly reloaded the Winchester, cocked the lever, and stood up.

He walked to the edge and jumped to the next summit, landed in a crouch, and remained motionless.

There was a noise behind him, and Murphy spun around as Quad jumped to a summit cloaked in the shadows of a higher peak.

Murphy fired the Winchester in the general direction where Quad had jumped and he heard Quad hit the ground and roll. That gave Murphy the few seconds he needed to stand and follow Quad across to the next summit.

As Murphy hit the ground and rolled, several pistol shots fired, one nearly hitting him in the leg.

Murphy ducked into the shadows behind a large rock and listened for a moment and he heard Quad jump to a new location.

Quad was close enough to use the Schofield pistol and he had fired three rounds. The problem with reloading it was that all six rounds needed to be fired to open the break because the spring action automatically ejected all six and not just the three that were fired.

Murphy rolled out from behind the rock and the moonlight illuminated Quad as he jumped across a summit to a higher point.

Murphy fired the Winchester and the shot hit the rocks close to Quad's face and he lost his footing and slid down the canyon into darkness.

Murphy had no choice but to follow Quad and ran fifty feet along the summit and then sat and slid down to the bottom.

He immediately rolled into the shadows of a large rock as three shots rang out and sparks of bullets striking rock flew by his head.

On the ground, Murphy listened to Quad open the Schofield pistol and eject the six spent shells. They fell to the ground and Murphy traced the location by sound. Quad was about twenty feet away, behind a jutting rock on the canyon floor.

Murphy silently cocked the lever of the Winchester and aimed it at the rock.

He heard the distinctive clink of the Schofield snapping back into place after being fully loaded.

Murphy held his aim.

Quad moved out from behind the rock. He was cloaked in darkness, but the slight movement of shadow moving against rock gave his location away and Murphy fired.

The Schofield fell from Quad's grasp as the bullet tore into Quad's left forearm.

Murphy cocked the Winchester and came out from hiding, but Quad was already gone. He ran to the rock and blood was on the surface and the Schofield pistol was on the ground.

Quad had gone up again.

Murphy looked up at the canyon wall. The rocks and cliffs appeared pale white in the moonlight.

He turned and walked to the opposite canyon wall some twenty feet apart. He chose a path in shadow and climbed to the summit.

He chose a large rock to take shelter

behind and balanced the Winchester on the rock, facing the opposite canyon summit.

The moon was at full crest and the summit floor was bright enough to read by. Quad had to be hiding behind a rock or peak.

Murphy gathered some pebbles off the floor and looked to his right. He tossed a few pebbles about ten feet away.

He kept his eyes on the shadows.

Then Murphy tossed some pebbles about twenty feet to his right.

On the opposite summit there was some shadow on shadow movement, but it was too dark to risk a shot.

Murphy tossed a few pebbles thirty feet to his right.

He watched the shadow in shadow movement on the opposite summit and brought the Winchester to his right eye and held the aim.

Then there it was.

The moonlight reflecting off the metal plate on the side of the Sharps rifle in Quad's hands.

Murphy calculated the shot, and fired slightly above the glowing plate.

The noise of the round echoed loudly inside the canyon walls. Murphy watched the Sharps rifle slide down the canyon wall and disappear into darkness at the bottom.

Murphy lowered the Winchester and watched as Quad appeared from the shadows and stood upright and looked up at the moon as if seeing it for the last time. Then he gasped and pitched forward and rolled down to the canyon floor.

Murphy slid down as fast as he could and found Quad on the bottom. Quad's left lung had been pierced by Murphy's bullet and he didn't have long left. Murphy sat beside Quad.

Quad motioned to Murphy with his hand and Murphy took it in his and Quad squeezed tightly.

"How?" Quad gasped.

"I covered the metal plate with mud," Murphy said. "Yours reflected moonlight."

Quad nodded.

"Will you give me peace?" Quad whispered.

"If I can."

"Take me home to Ohio, and bury me with my wife and child on the family farm."

"I will," Murphy said. "You have my word."

Quad nodded, and then closed his eyes.

He died a little while later holding Murphy's hand.

THIRTY-TWO

The Quad family farm in Ohio hadn't been worked in many years. Quad's parents were buried in a small plot of land surrounded by a yellow picket fence. Quad's wife and baby were buried beside them.

Murphy smoked his pipe while he watched the four gravediggers he hired slowly lower Quad's casket into the grave beside Quad's wife and baby.

A minister who knew the Quad family spoke a few parting words over the grave.

Murphy left the small cemetery and walked to the deserted farmhouse where Boyle waited for him.

Before he mounted Boyle, Murphy took a look around at the land, at the overgrown fields and rotting house and barns. It wasn't that hard to imagine a family living and working here, sharing the evening meal, laughing and going to church in town on Sunday before the war started and tore things apart.

He mounted Boyle and rode to the town of Rayfield near the Ohio/West Virginia border to mail the letter he wrote to Quad's sister, Reeva, in Colorado.

THIRTY-THREE

Burke met Murphy at the train station in Washington DC. Murphy led Boyle from the boxcar to the waiting area and found Burke seated in his open carriage.

Burke stepped down from the carriage when Murphy approached him.

"You've done a man's job, sir," Burke said. "And the President is very grateful to you for ending the hostilities against the railroad."

Murphy nodded as he prepared to mount Boyle.

"Where are you going?" Burke said. "I have orders to bring you to the White House. Garfield wants to thank you personally and for you to have dinner with him."

"Tell him I'll see him for dinner tonight," Murphy said and mounted Boyle. "I need a shave, a bath, and a change of clothes."

"Yes, of course," Burke said. "I'll tell him that. Dinner is at seven-thirty."

Murphy nodded and rode away from the station.

"To hell with Congress," Garfield said. "You're the best damn regulator in the business. You'll work directly for me and take on special assignments that require your unique talents."

They were having dinner in Garfield's private dining room. Once the meal had been served, Garfield dismissed the servants so they could talk openly.

"I need to go home to Tennessee and see my family," Murphy said. "And then to Saint Louis to see a woman I've met."

"When will you leave?" Garfield said.

"Tomorrow by train."

"I will be leaving in a week for Williams College to give a speech," Garfield said. "Plan on meeting with me in one month."

"Yes, sir," Murphy said.

"Let's have dessert and coffee in the gardens," Garfield said. "It's a beautiful evening."

Murphy stood before the small cemetery on his Tennessee farm and looked at the headstones for his wife and child.

"I'm not ready to quit on life just yet, Katherine," he said aloud. "Sally is what good southern gentlemen would call common, but she has a joy for life that I need, so with your permission I will pay her a visit."

Thirty-six hours later, Murphy stood on the curb outside the building where Madam Orr housed her business. The building was a three-story red brick structure with cement steps and a frosted glass door protected by black iron bars.

He climbed the steps and pulled the cord hanging beside the door and chimes sounded from inside the house.

It took a minute or more for the door to be answered. The glass door opened but the iron bars did not.

A large man in a black suit looked at Murphy through the bars.

"I'm here to see Sally Orr," Murphy said.

"Your name?"

"Tell her it's Murphy come to keep a promise."

Epilogue

Two days later, Sally and Murphy had breakfast on the third floor balcony overlooking the backyard gardens. The balcony led to her private residence of four large rooms.

Sally wore a robe over a sheer nightgown to the breakfast table. Her hair was down and surprisingly long. She wore no makeup. Murphy thought she didn't need any.

As she sipped coffee from an expensive cup, Sally said, "How is this going to work?"

"What?" Murphy said.

"I can't exactly live in Washington," Sally said. "Quite a few senators and congressmen have passed through my doors on trips to Saint Louis over the years."

"Who said anything about living in Washington?"

"Where?"

"Tennessee."

"I can't, and won't, live with ghosts," Sally

said. "I told you that."

"No ghosts," Murphy said. "Just the living."

Sally nodded. "So how can you report to the President living a thousand miles away?"

"I'll have telegraph wires installed at the farmhouse," Murphy said.

"And exactly what does a regulator do for the President?"

"Whatever he needs done."

There was a soft knock on the bedroom door and Sally stood, entered the bedroom, and returned a moment later with a newspaper.

"I think what he needs done you can't deliver," Sally said.

"What do you mean?"

Sally set the newspaper on the table where Murphy read the bold headline.

**President Garfield shot by assassin
in route to Williams College.**

ABOUT THE AUTHOR

Ethan J. Wolfe is a native of New York City. He has traveled and studied the American West extensively. He is the author of the novels *The Last Ride* and *The Regulator.* He is presently working on the second novel in the Regulator series.